Alice S. Wolf

A house of cards

Alice S. Wolf

A house of cards

ISBN/EAN: 9783743306332

Manufactured in Europe, USA, Canada, Australia, Japa

Cover: Foto ©Andreas Hilbeck / pixelio.de

Manufactured and distributed by brebook publishing software
(www.brebook.com)

Alice S. Wolf

A house of cards

A House of Cards

BY

ALICE S. WOLF

CHICAGO

STONE & KIMBALL

M DCCC XCVI

TO MY MOTHER

A House of Cards.

———◆———

Chapter I.

RIKER VAN ARSDALE drew a chair within the embrasured club-window, and let his gaze wander out upon the mellow splendor of the night.

The rooms behind him wore a deserted air. It was the week of the annual shoot of the Country Club at Del Monte, and those members who were in town had not yet left the dining-tables.

Van Arsdale had not lingered over the meal: he had chanced to dine with a man who could not forget to remember who he was.

Presently his solitude was invaded by a man who leaned against the window-frame, smiling down upon him.

"Poor Van," began the new-comer, "I wonder you can look so cheerful after that irksome hour.   When I saw you cornered by Ives, I pitied you."

"That was kind of you, Kendall," commented the older man, no trace of sarcasm in his quiet tones.

"Did you manage to pierce the brazen wall of his ignorance?" asked Kendall, with gentle malice.

He was a broad-shouldered man, of average height, and the only fault Van Arsdale found with his face was that it was too handsome ; but all of Gregory Kendall's faults were pleasant ones, and his friends willingly adopted an easy attitude toward his shortcomings.

"I did not try to do so.   I found his self-sufficiency refreshing in these days when we are all inclined to thrust the analytical scalpel under our every thought and act."

"At any rate, you must have been bored."

"You forget : I am never bored," corrected Van Arsdale.

"Well, it bores me to dine here," volunteered Kendall.   "I came to-night only because I promised to dine with my father before he starts for Carlsbad.   All they do here is to eat and gamble."

A pause ensued, in which Van Arsdale continued to look across at the shadowy plaza, and Kendall twisted his mustache ruthlessly. At length Van Arsdale spoke; his eyes were still fixed upon the wavering trees.

" You were going to speak to me of — "

" Don't be clairvoyant to-night. I shall reach my point soon enough. It would be easier to speak if I did not stand in fear of your verdict. You know you have a truly reprehensible, inconsiderate habit of telling the truth."

Van Arsdale's acute ears detected the note of nervousness in the light words.

" I may have an inconvenient love for the truth, but I realize it is much too sacred to be tampered with ordinarily. I indulge in it only on those occasions when, at all hazards, I must be disbelieved. Now that you have warned me, I promise to be discreet. I shall slake your unconquerable thirst for sympathy, and advise only those things I shall see you are determined to do. It is always gratifying to see one's counsel followed."

To give Kendall an opportunity to collect himself, Van Arsdale had spoken at greater length than was his wont.

He was an habitually taciturn man; yet when

people presumed upon him they were apt to discover that his wit was singularly poignant, though hidden under a quiet exterior: he could utter very disagreeable truths in his calmly courteous way. But he was most trying when he said nothing, merely looking through his companion, at the back of his chair. Men invariably liked him, and thought he might be attractive to women if he only permitted his face to show more interest in them. Women admired him, — at a distance generally, for he cared little for their society. His friends were intimate with Van Arsdale; Van Arsdale was intimate with no one. Gregory Kendall rightly or wrongly imagined himself one of his most intimate friends, and it cost a great deal to be Kendall's friend. He usually opened an account about which there was no reciprocity.

Van Arsdale, in his position as manager of a large insurance company, had found it possible to assist Kendall in his career of the law, and he became accustomed to helping him in other ways. He had long since discovered that doing a man one kindness leaves you open to his importunities on all occasions, and that gratitude is only "a lively sense of future favors."

"Well," commenced Kendall, half-tremulously, half-defiantly, "I hope your advice will coincide with my views, for even if it does not, I intend — "

"This is novel," interposed Van Arsdale, throwing his hands about his head. "There is not even a feint of humility about you; and usually we confessors are beguiled by the outward meekness of those who approach us. Proceed with your piquant confidences."

With most of his little world, Kendall stood in wholesome fear of Van Arsdale's censure. He had always felt proud of the friendship, and now he found it difficult to frame his sentences.

"I am going to be married," he finally announced, in a tone at once combative and appealing.

"Yes?" murmured Van Arsdale, his inscrutable face betraying no emotion of any kind. It was a face of which one never gained a clear impression, although the features were sharply cut. A more observant man than Kendall might have noticed that his eyes narrowed unpleasantly, and that his mouth grew a trifle more set and stern.

"You might say something," broke forth

Kendall, "instead of looking the embodiment of virtuous disapproval."

"I really beg pardon. You see I did not know what you expected me to say. It was very remiss, but it is not too late to hope you will know all happiness." He did not unclasp his hands from about his head. "When do you get married?"

Kendall's handsome face turned a shade whiter.

"What a fool you make a man look! Possibly I should have said I intend to get married if Miss Yerrington will have me."

"Perhaps it would have been a more conservative measure, if you are not yet engaged," assented Van Arsdale, in his unhurried tones.

"I do not know why I am annoying you with the matter, for I think that in my heart I realize she will not have me," proceeded Kendall. "She is a great deal too good for me."

"Of course," granted Van Arsdale.

Kendall laughed shortly. "Yes, I suppose they all say that. Well, I am not disheartened, although Loys has been refusing me ever since I was twenty-six, and that was five years ago.

I tell her that some day she will grow so weary of saying ' No,' that she will change it into a ' Yes.' "

" Did Miss Yerrington go to the Yosemite, as she had planned?" queried Van Arsdale, with a courteous show of interest.

" If you remember, she said she had little hope of it," prompted Kendall, "and the little she had died an untimely death. She went to the farm, and is passing an interminable vacation."

" No doubt she will find time for a great deal of writing, and she must need the perfect rest."

" One would not choose the Yerrington farm as a haven of rest ; and she is nursing her father through a fever. She will return wan and exhausted. She is occupied from early morning until late at night, and the hopeless dreariness of the life is maddening to her."

" I understood that Mr. Yerrington was a man of wealth."

" His place adjoins ours, so I know the length and breadth of his possessions : the land he owns is worth over one hundred thousand dollars," returned Kendall; "but of money he has none. Whatever he clears is invested in

new purchases of land, so the money Loys
sends him every month is more than welcome.
I am counting on all this to win for me in the
end," he concluded frankly.

Van Arsdale volunteered no remark.

"What was your impression of Loys?"

"That she is not a woman one can sum up
and dismiss in an epigram, and I have met her
but the once," Van Arsdale reminded. "And
perhaps, even were I tempted to tell you what I
think of her, I should refrain, for I realize that
my opinion must be biased. It is impossible
not to be prejudiced against one who unkindly
thinks that I remind her of a lead-pencil, with
a rubber at the end of it."

The suspicion of a smile curved his lips.
He thought he had never heard a briefer, more
exact description of his appearance, and he
appreciated the discernment of the woman who
had made it.

Kendall laughingly eyed the long, gaunt
figure of his friend. "I should not have repeated her words; but when you seemed so
curious to learn what she had said, and plainly
fancied you were to hear some critical analysis
of your character, I could not resist the temptation. Besides, I knew it would please your

sense of humor. You will wish me luck?" he pleaded.

For the first time Van Arsdale faced him.

"You love her?" he commenced.

"I think my life since I have known her will be my best answer," returned Kendall, simply.

"I believe so too. Then you love her enough to renounce all thought of her as your wife," affirmed Van Arsdale, rising, and placing his hand on his friend's shoulder.

Kendall shook himself free. "Why don't you say you think me a coward, and be done with it?" he demanded.

"Because you warned me against such a drastic course," Van Arsdale confessed a trifle wearily, resuming his seat.

An uncomfortable pause ensued ; then Kendall went on with an unsuccessful effort at easiness : "The members of the Round Table are already talking of the affair they intend to give Yorke. Do you suppose he has left anything for other explorers to discover?"

"I cannot tell. I am content to know he did not set out on the last voyage of discovery, as was rumored."

Kendall joined a group of men who had just entered. Some moments later Van Arsdale

2

recognized him as he boarded a passing cable-car. Van Arsdale continued to sit before the open window some time longer.

"There is nothing to fear," he ultimately decided. "Kendall himself realizes it is only a forlorn hope. Miss Yerrington is wrapped up in her desire to drink of the enchanted wine of fame — she does not think of marriage. If she were to marry him, she would deserve the misery which would surely be hers; but I fancy she is one of those intense women, with a nascent taste for martyrdom: she would never permit him to suspect her wretchedness. She would be an interesting study. If she loved Kendall, it would be bad enough; for I imagine she would find it difficult to accept calmly the fact that a man can be only a man. As it is — she will not marry him. She has known Kendall too many years not to know — . And she is a woman with an exaggerated sense of responsibility."

"I believe," he confided to himself, with a certain amusement at his own folly, "I believe I have been troubling over some one's else affairs."

Chapter II.

THE parched ground gaped thirstily under the sullen glare of the sun beating fiercely down from the low-hanging sky. The dense heat of the mid-day seemed only emphasized by the leafy shadows of the few ross-grown trees which stood in the lately-harvested, out-lying fields. The raucous note of a belligerent cock broke discordantly on the heavy air.

Andrew Yerrington walked up the gravelled path, noting with vigilant eyes the blistering paint of the farm buildings. He took down the small feather duster which hung beside the house-door, and waving it across his dusty boots, walked into the dining-room.

The majority of the farm-hands had already eaten, but three or four of them had just entered, and were being served by Laura and Nora Yerrington.

"W'ar 's yer sister?" Yerrington demanded, shortly.

His daughters looked at each other helplessly, the one relying upon the other to answer. Finally Laura said, "Ma's helping her pack. She says she does n't want any dinner."

"Yeh tell Loys I don't want no more er her fulishness. She's ter kum eat her dinnur this instunt." He spoke with the unpleasant deliberation it sometimes pleased him to assume. It was at those times Andrew Yerrington was most feared.

He continued to eat on stolidly. Loys Yerrington was to return to San Francisco that afternoon, and, while he was conscious that he should draw a breath of relief at her departure, he also realized that he should miss her. She added zest to his life. He could remember the time when his wife had been much the same as Loys; now, with a darkening brow, he characterized her as a poor meek creature, and the other girls were like her. He had bent them to his iron will, and in the end he was displeased with his work. He liked a woman, as well as a horse, to have a little "spirrut." Loys had escaped him. She dared to think for herself, and even sat in judgment on him.

He had offered his daughters the opportunity of a good education, but Loys was the only one who had availed herself of it. He had stormed when Gregory Kendall had secured Loys the position as teacher of English and history in Miss Eastlake's institute, but when her will had overridden his, he had stipulated that her salary should be forwarded to him each month. He felt he had a right to it; but sometimes, when he thought of the meagre "'lowunce" he made her, a swarthy flush flooded his cheeks, and he muttered, "Her spirrut 'ull hev ter be broke. She kin git more w'en she begs furrit."

Loys never "got more." She never begged for anything.

Mrs. Yerrington entered the room hurriedly. She glanced appealingly toward her husband, saying, "She 's comin', Andrew."

She nervously served herself, and endeavored to eat.

"Yeh 've ben doin' too much fer Loys, ma," remarked Yerrington, looking her over not unkindly, the while stroking the fringe of gray whisker which adorned his pointed chin.

"I could n't do anything for her. She was helping in the kitchen all morning, and I was afraid she 'd be late."

"Yeh don't need to be afeared fer Loys."

Loys Yerrington paused on the threshold. The stifling heat was rendered the more intolerable by the steam and the odors of the food. The family was now alone, and the two girls had sat down to eat without removing the empty dishes with which the table was laden.

Loys already had on her travelling-gown, which clung admirably to her perfectly-rounded figure. The heat had added to the creamy pallor of her face, and lent a touch of languor to her movements. She walked well, — a rare accomplishment. She appeared taller than she really was, which, perhaps, was due as much to her mode of arranging her wealth of hair as to her carriage.

"Yere's a chair," remarked Yerrington. "Tek sum berries, ef yeh don't hanker arter anythun more fillin'. It's most too hot ter eat, nohow. But yeh'll go all ter pieces ef yeh don't swaller sumthun."

Loys seated herself. A large coffee-stain on the table-cloth stared her in the face. Her father was stirring his tea so vigorously that the saucer was flooded.

"I'd s'posed yeh'd hev un yer bunnet. Natchelly, yer pinin' ter git back."

Nature had not taken into consideration the

possibilities of Yerrington's wishing to be face-
tious. He was at no time handsome, but he
was most unpleasant to look at when he smiled.
His thin lips parted painfully over his yellow
teeth and discolored gums; Loys was always
in dread lest the tightly drawn skin would
break.

He sipped the tea loudly through his closed
teeth, looking from Loys to her sisters.

"W'y don't yeh fix yer ha'r tidy like hern?"
he demanded of Laura.

"I have n't got the time, pa," she answered,
good-naturedly.

"We 're ull druv yere," he allowed. "We 'ns
ain't got no time ter mek oursels pooty.
P'r'aps it 's jest ez well. I allers like ter see a
gyrl look sorter genteel, but they ez sech a thun
ez her carin' too much fer perkin' up. They 's
thet shameless hussy's picter in yer room,
Loys. Ef I hed my way, I 'd hev burned it. A
painted Jezebel, 'thout enuff close un. Mebby
it seems ull right ter yeh now, fer yeh hev
grow'd slack; but onct un a time it 'd hev
seemed ull wrong."

Loys played with her spoon, her eyes discreetly veiled. She would be tempted into no
argument. It would all be over in another hour.

"W'y don't yeh ansur?   'T aint likely yeh agree with me."

"No, I do not agree with you."

"Yeh ain't got nothun agin it, then.   Yeh think it's decent?"

"I wonder if you ever heard a story I once came across about your friend Dr. Johnson."

"I ain't never heerd tell un it."

"He was standing before a statue with Boswell," commenced the girl, "and Boswell asked him if he did not think it indecent. 'No, sir,' was the reply, 'but your remark is.'"

There was an ominous silence as she finished. Her father bent upon her his angry eyes, which she met calmly.   She wished she had not spoken, but the words seemed to have been forced from her.   Before Yerrington could speak, Gregory Kendall stood within the room.

"I'll hev ter mek tracks," said Yerrington. "They's a passel er work ter be done afore night-fall, and I s'pose yeh want sumbuddy ter tek yeh and yer vallisses to the station."

"Let me save you the trouble," put in Kendall.   "I shall be glad to take Loys, if she is willing."

"Thank you, Gregory," interposed Loys. "Nora promised to drive me to the station."

"They ain't no sense in mekin' the trip ef Kendall's goin'. It's hot out, red hot, and Nora and the hoss'u'd kum back tuckered out. Yeh kin jest ez well go with him," insisted Yerrington.

He gave an unsatisfactory peck at his daughter's cheek, and passed from the house. The fragrance of her face haunted him. The care she took of herself was sinful, he thought, but he liked the contact with her violet-scented cheek.

Loys went upstairs, followed by her mother. Mrs. Yerrington watched her put on her hat and veil, her lips pressed together as if to restrain a moan.

"It's hard to think I won't see you until Christmas," she began.

The girl knelt down beside her, bringing the madly swaying rocker to a sudden stand-still.

"It would be so easy for you to come, mother dear. If it were only for a few days, I should be content. You don't know what happiness we should crowd into those days. Promise to come."

She pressed her cheek against her mother's faded one; she clasped the work-stained hands in_her own exquisitely modelled ones. The

only point of resemblance between them was
the eyes.   There was the same soft appeal in
both, but Loys's were the more intelligent, and
her imperious mouth denied their gentleness.

Mrs. Yerrington's lips moved convulsively.
"Your father, dear, he would n't like it.   No, it
can't be," she decided.

"Why should he be so cruel?" rebelled the
girl.

"Hush, child.   Your father is a good man,
and a forgivin' one.   Don't you ever think him
harsh."

The mother always upheld the father before
the child.   Loys respected her all the more for
it.   Before her husband, Mrs. Yerrington never
showed Loys any affection; when they were
alone, she could not altogether restrain the outburst of her tenderness.   Her other daughters
would have looked upon any mark of affection
as a waste of time.   She was their mother, and,
naturally, they loved her; there was no need to
say anything about it.

"Mother, do you know you have forgotten
that I am twenty-four years old to-day?"

"I quite forgot; I don't see how I did, but I
forgot.   But your father remembered.   He told
me to give you this.   He must have remem-

bered it was your birthday; he never forgets it," she whispered, as if to herself, straining Loys's hands with fierce intensity. "And I clean forgot. It does n't seem as if it could be twenty-four years ago." She forced into the girl's unwilling hands an envelope, which evidently contained money. "Don't you refuse it, Loys, for my sake. I wish you — "

Loys folded her arms about her mother. There was a mistiness about their eyes when Loys drew on her gloves.

"I wish your father had let Nora take you to the station, since you'd have preferred it. Listen, Loys: don't marry Gregory, if you don't love him. I don't see how you could well do better; but don't take him, if you don't love him."

"Gregory knows, mother, that I shall never marry him."

She went into the kitchen to bid the Chinese cook good-by, then kissed her sisters.

In a way they were sorry to see her go. She was quick and willing, and made their work light for them; but they also knew that they could lapse into modes of speech and habits at which Loys openly frowned. Altogether, it was more comfortable when she was away.

Loys and Kendall were alone in the dog-cart. The pitiless glare of the brazen sun was insupportable, but Loys was unconscious of it. She was absorbed in her shamed feeling of relief at getting away. Kendall looked down upon her, — a great happiness in his eyes because he was with her.

"Of what are you thinking, Loys?" he asked.

She was looking over at Mount Diablo in the distance, a tremulous smile upon her lips.

"I have been indulging myself in a little cheap cynicism. Do you remember when we took this drive together four years ago, when I first went to Miss Eastlake's? I wonder that you did not laugh at my audacious confidence in myself. I believed " — she hurried on, with a mirthless little laugh — " Ah, what did I not believe? But now I have grown so sceptical I do not even believe in myself."

"I wish I could impart to you some of my content."

"Contentment is a diet on which one turns into a vegetable. I do not wish to be content with what I have."

"Most women would be content with what you have," he urged. "You live —"

"No, I do not; and as long as I live, I wish to live. For four years I have been describing the same circle; but perhaps, during three of them, it was with the hope that the circle would widen. I had dreams of success and travel. And now, now I know I shall rise every morning (before I have any inclination to rise) to teach history and English, to go to bed so exhausted that I shall have no desire to improve myself. There is no sense in denying it, — poverty is a strait-jacket, and one it is impossible to wrest open. I am afraid I am growing to be a professional pessimist," she added, ruefully.

It was not often she made a confidant of him, for she realized that he could not understand or sympathize with her wild dreams and vaulting ambitions.

"Would you marry for money?" he queried.

"Oh, no, I was taught that I was not to do that; but I am equally as determined not to fall in love with any but a wealthy man. A woman's heart is such an accommodating article. It will be a case of, —

> 'I would not love you half so much, dear,
> Loved I not riches more.'"

She turned to Kendall, making a show of gravity; and he, noting her mouth of exquisite sensibility, decided that she meant nothing of what she had said.

"So you think you would be happy if you could travel?" he questioned, looking between the horse's ears.

"Happy? I do not know. But I do not wish to go out of the world having seen nothing of it. Ah, well, if I do, I warn you, I shall come back as a ghost-*ess*, to wander about all the splendors I am now missing."

By a mental pirouette she had regained the safety of the middle course. On the instant she became more tangible to him.

"Loys," he whispered, "I have not much to offer you, but I would do my utmost to make you happy. Is it — "

"Don't," she pleaded. "We have been through it all a great many times before, and it will always have the same ending. Don't you see, dear, that I could do without all of which I spoke, if I loved you? But I do not, and I never shall."

"I wonder what I would have said," she mused, as she stepped from the cart, "if he had asked me to be his wife when we first left

the farm.   I am glad I do not know.   I was so
anxious to get away from the sordidness of it all.
Fortunately he never asks me when I am in one
of my moods."

In her interest in the flying landscape, Kendall was soon dismissed from her thoughts.

own recognition, and she would have been in a
fair way to be spoiled had not her native
good sense saved her. She had never, unfortunately, been able to deceive herself, and the
world met with no greater success.

For more than a year she watched the antics
of her little circle with a spice of amused
malice; then its jejune conversation began
to bore her seriously, and, having served her
novitiate, she rarely afterward ventured beyond
the frontiers of society.

Under the chaperonage of Mrs. Luttrell, an
old family friend, she travelled extensively, and
had only within the week returned to San
Francisco from Japan.

"I hope Wilson will not announce dinner
just yet," Penelope was saying, as she stood in
her drawing-room that evening, with Mrs.
Luttrell, Riker Van Arsdale, and Laura Yorke,
a school-girl of eighteen or nineteen years of
age. "Bishop makes it a point to dine with
me on my birthday, even at some inconvenience
to himself; consequently I shall feel wounded
if he allows the matter of a few hundred miles
to keep him away to-night."

She moved across the room to arrange some
lilies, and Laura Yorke noted the exquisite

detail of her toilet. Penelope Browning achieved the by no means easy triumph, for a woman with unlimited means at her command, of having her clothes impress the onlooker, not with a desire to know how much they cost, but where she ordered them.

" But, you see," interposed Laura Yorke, " he returned only last Wednesday, when he joined mother at Castle Crag. As she expects to return to-morrow, it is not probable he will be here to-night."

She was speaking of Bishop Yorke, her half-brother. She somewhat resented Penelope's calm belief that he would disarrange all his plans merely for the sake of dining with her that night. No trace of her annoyance was visible, however.

As the last word died away, Yorke was announced.

He stood for a second looking about him, as though pleased to find himself again in the room, then crossed to Mrs. Luttrell, while his strong bronzed face relaxed into a smile of undisguised pleasure.

He was a distinctly noticeable man in appearance.. The lower portion of his face, however, was of such marked vigor of outline that it tended to produce an impression of strength rather than of beauty. Some people chose to consider him too tall; but when he stood next to other men, he never appeared awkward, — they only seemed insignificant. The room seemed suddenly to have grown smaller.

"It was kind of you to wait for me; I see in the action your faith in me," he murmured, as he bent over Penelope's hand.

He turned to greet his sister, who said, " I did not expect you until to-morrow. Did mamma return with you?"

"No," he returned, smiling leisurely down at her. "I was sorry to leave her, but she will be quite comfortable under the care of her maid, and I always contrive, if possible, to dine with Penelope on this night."

Her eyes fell under his gaze. She was angered that she had revealed her jealousy of his attention to their hostess.

"And so you have concluded to spend the winter in Italy," Yorke hazarded, when his first hunger had been appeased.

"Yes, and then to continue on a systematic voyage of discovery," Penelope explained. "I feel I am unkind to entail upon Mrs. Luttrell all the fatigue of sight-seeing. It is time that she be relieved. Do you know some in-teresting, charming woman who would be willing to accompany us?"

"It is 'time that Mrs. Luttrell be relieved," agreed Van Arsdale.

"Yes, it is time," echoed Yorke, discreetly lowering his lids to conceal a smile.

Penelope Browning's lips parted in a smile of amusement. "It was very clever of you," she commenced, turning to Van Arsdale. "I con-fess I was surprised at the size of the bunch, and proceeded suspiciously to count the roses you sent me to-day. There were twenty-five full-blown, feathery flowers, and one tiny bud. They were symbolical of my years. I smiled appreciatively."

"And twenty-five and one make twenty-six," reminded Laura.

"Ah," breathed Penelope, making a careful scrutiny of Laura's cold face, "Ah, I was never clever at figures. It was a thing to which little attention was given in my school-days. I am not a calculating young woman, Laura. And yet the sight of the roses filled me with a vague dismay. I held my hand-mirror in the clear, disheartening light, and realized, with cruel keenness, that it is time, as you so pleasantly intimate, that I arrange myself. It must be a very superior article which can go through twenty-five years of this weary strife and still show no signs of wear and tear. But all my faculties are, as yet, unimpaired, — that of speech in particular."

"Yes, it is time," reiterated Riker Van Arsdale. "A woman never attains her true happiness until she is married. The frame of your mind, Penelope, is clearly indicated by your unsettled mode of life. You are forever on the wing — "

"Pursuing happiness," she interrupted.

"I think we both came to-night, prepared to make you realize the folly of your course," declared Yorke. "We are such old friends, we feel we have the right to speak quite openly, for you have always granted us that privilege. You are such a womanly woman, I know you will find your happiness only in your home and husband."

"Don't wait too long," cautioned Van Arsdale. "Each year you will grow more exacting."

"And we must learn to close our eyes, or else peer discreetly between our fingers at the failings of our fellows," put in Yorke.

Penelope raised her glass and drank almost

feverishly, then bent her head toward Van
Arsdale.

"Have you no conception of your foolhardi-
ness?" she demanded, her long eyes narrowing.
"You have planted the idea of marriage in my
active imagination. You have even held it out
to me as a duty, and no one ever knew me to
avoid a duty. Yet you must have been alive
to the fact that you two are the men I like best.
You have planned your own Frankenstein. Be-
ware that it does not destroy you."

Van Arsdale's worn smile flickered across
his face and died prematurely. Yorke flushed
uncomfortably under her gay tone. Possibly
they had overstepped the bounds of good
taste by speaking so plainly, although she had
always encouraged them to do so. In former
years the comments of to-night had been spoken
in jest; but possibly it was the strain of earnest-
ness which now offended.

"Shall I tell you why I am not married?"
she asked.

They all bent upon her a look of mock
serious attention, and Mrs. Luttrell laughed at
the grave import of her words.

"It all happened years ago," — Penelope
began, in a musing voice, — "so long ago that I

forget when it first came to me — Love. You must not blame the man; he made no effort to win it. And ever since he has filled entirely the niche in my heart."

She looked before her at the yellow roses, now beginning to droop their proud heads, and Laura Yorke foolishly wondered if she knew how beautiful she looked as the candles' dim light brought out the warm glints of her brown hair and deepened the shadows under her softened eyes. Her expression of inflexible gravity stilled their indecent laughter.

"Why do you not marry him?" asked Laura.

"Why?" echoed Penelope. "Why, because he does not love me."

Mrs. Luttrell laughed outright in amusement. It was too ridiculous to see Penelope's pose.

"Are you quite certain?" queried Yorke, falling in with her humor, and admiring the skill with which she was playing her rôle.

"Quite certain," she answered, simply.

"Does he know?" inquired Mrs. Luttrell.

Penelope started. "I think not. No, no; of course not."

"Then let him know," counselled the older woman.

The girl smiled proudly, and drew herself up.

"Put him out of your heart, then, and be happy. with another man," suggested Yorke, taking a peach.

"And what do you advise?" Penelope asked, turning to Van Arsdale.

"To wait. He is alive, and unmarried? Yes. I prophesy success for you. It is better to wait for the one, even if he never comes, than to make a pretence of happiness with another."

"I think so too," she affirmed. Then, to her surprise as well as theirs, a tear gathered in her eye, and glistened there unheeded. No one appeared to see it. "I shall wait, and yet I know I shall wait in vain. Let us forget my melancholy history."

She watched Yorke with unlimited curiosity as he disposed of his peach.

"You deserve a round of applause," she continued; "for a peach is the most difficult thing to eat gracefully. As the two dear old souls in 'Cranford' ate their oranges in the privacy of their own rooms, because the juice ran everywhere, do you suppose they ate their peaches leaning over a fence?"

"Miss Yerrington said that very thing to me yesterday," observed Laura Yorke.

"Who is Miss Yerrington?" appealed Mrs. Luttrell.

"The teacher of history and English literature at Miss Eastlake's," responded Laura.

"You are very fortunate to be under her," Van Arsdale volunteered. "She is an unusual young woman."

They looked at him in faint surprise.

"I met Miss Yerrington through Kendall," he explained, in reply to Penelope's slightly arched brows. "They are great friends."

"Gregory Kendall," repeated Penelope. "It seems strange to think of him as the friend of one of Miss Eastlake's teachers. I thought he never knew any one not possessed of a million or two."

"I never noticed that characteristic in Kendall," remonstrated Yorke, "though I should not blame him for it. Life is a game of whist, and it is part of one's duties to know who holds trumps and diamonds and the high honors."

"That she is young is an innovation," resumed Penelope, taking Yorke's rebuke with the calm of one accustomed to his reprimands. "In other days, all of Miss Eastlake's teachers were so old, it seemed that death had forgotten them. So she teaches you English, which I suppose she don't know herself."

"Yes, she do," contradicted Laura. "Oh, I did not intend to be rude!"

"Why do you say 'She do,' and then color so warmly?"

"You see, you said, 'She don't,' and when we say that, Miss Yerrington interrupts quietly, 'Oh, yes, she do.' We say 'She does n't,' now."

The smile became epidemic.

"She writes," put in Van Arsdale. "Perhaps you read that story of hers on Saturday, — 'A Last Resource.'"

"Was that hers? It was told with fine dramatic power, and was extremely well written," commended Yorke.

"Name us some of her heroes in history," directed Penelope.

Laura knit her brows. "I do not know her, or her likes or dislikes, intimately. Still, I think she admires Napoleon vastly, for her voice rings as she quotes, 'Carelessly, almost in a stooping attitude, rode the Emperor, with one hand holding aloft the rein, with the other stroking in kindly fashion his horse's neck. It was a sunny, marble hand, a —'"

"— mighty hand, one of those two hands

that had bound the many-headed monster of anarchy, and enforced order amidst the conflict of the nations ; and now it was caressing good-naturedly the mane of his horse," supplied Yorke, in German, as Laura faltered. " His face too had the sheen that we notice in the countenances of Greek and Roman statues; its features certainly were cast in the noble mould of the antique, and on them was written, ' Thou shalt have no other gods before me.' "

"Does she know Heine in the original?" queried Penelope.

"Yes, and do you know why she is studying French now?" Laura paused abruptly, as if dismayed at her own prolixity.

"And why is she studying French?" asked Yorke, encouragingly.

It was too late for retreat. The look of confusion still lingered, but the girl was smiling as she continued, " One evening when I was not well, and she was bathing my head (no one has such a hand as Miss Yerrington), she told me she was studying French that she might speak it to her children, and save them the necessity of struggling with the difficulties of the language."

Yorke's laugh led all the rest.

Van Arsdale was the last to leave that night. As he and Penelope stood in the drawing-room, she said: "I have been thinking of Laura's Miss Yerrington. I fancy I should like her. Do you think she would be willing to go away with us?"

"I have no doubt you would like her, and that she would be glad to accompany you," he returned. "I think you would be peculiarly well-fitted for each other."

"Upon your return from Alaska, will you take me to her?"

"I do not know her well enough for that. Gregory Kendall will take you."

"Oh, I thought you knew her very well. We shall be in Southern California nearly two months, but I shall not forget her, and when we return Gregory must take me to her."

Although she had a retentive memory, she carefully made a memorandum to write to Kendall while at Coronado.

On the following afternoon Yorke brought to his sister a rare first edition of "The Book Le Grand," which contained a verse in Heine's own hand.

"Will you give this to Miss Yerrington?" he said. "I am glad to send it to one who will

appreciate it.   This card will make the acceptance very easy."

He had skillfully worded the note so as
to exact an answer, and when he heard that
Miss Yerrington had accepted the book, he
watched for her acknowledgment with an
eagerness which diverted even himself.   But
none ever came.

Chapter IV.

IT was approaching the close of study-hour in Miss Eastlake's institute.

Loys Yerrington sympathized with the girls that evening in their only half-concealed distaste for their books. It had been one of those sultry, enervating days that visit San Francisco in September, but now, through the open windows, there swept the refreshing night-breezes which seemed to woo them from the gas-lit rooms.

The majority of Miss Eastlake's patrons were day-pupils; Laura Yorke was the only one, residing in San Francisco, who boarded at the school.

She was now leaning her fair, unruffled head on her hand, watching Kate Tisdall, who was still pondering over the morrow's lessons.

In San Francisco it is, generally, only the wealthiest class which sends its children to the private schools. After a more than usually irk-

some day, Loys Yerrington would affirm to
herself whimsically that she believed in the law
of compensation.   Had Miss Eastlake's pupils
been less wealthy, they might have been in
danger of being termed oafs.

Loys glanced resentfully at the clock, which
seemed to sparkle with malicious pleasure at
so slowly marking off the minutes.   Laura
Yorke's eyes fell upon her.   She could not
remember ever having seen Miss Yerrington
look so unutterably weary.

"What a fool she is, to waste her time on
these idiots !" mused the girl.   "Why does n't
she marry Gregory Kendall, and get away from
it all?   The great reason why she is so dissatis-
fied is that she has not the time to write.   If
she were married, she could do as she liked.
I wonder if she is foolish enough to dream of
a King Cophetua in this Nineteenth Century
of ours."

Kate Tisdall closed her books with a sigh of
relief, and, glancing at Miss Yerrington, turned
to Laura with a shrug of the shoulders which
indicated that they were unobserved.   School-
girls always have their fingers clasped tightly
around their teacher's pulse.

"I have learned of the grandest fortune-teller," Kate began, in a penetrating whisper. "Cousin Mary says she is simply wonderful. She just takes your hands in hers and then reveals your past and your fu—"

"Only one class of people goes to fortune-tellers," broke in Laura, decisively. "I am surprised that Mrs. Herrick should have gone. I imagined only servants and people of that stamp displayed a vulgar curiosity about the future."

"Oh, do they?" scoffed her companion. "Why, all the physicians and lawyers in town think this Mrs. Wills wonderful. Cousin Mary told me that nearly all of these clairvoyants are illiterate frauds, but that Mrs. Wills is extremely intelligent. You ought to hear the things she told Cousin Mary. Would n't you like to go this Saturday? We can manage it some way."

"It might be interesting as an experience," deliberated Laura. "Madame de Pompadour's future was foretold when she was only ten, and so was Eugénie's, and—"

"Miss Yorke!" called Loys, warningly.

Five minutes later she dismissed the girls, but requested Laura Yorke and Kate Tisdall to remain.

4

"I had no objection to your whispering," she commenced, "for I knew you would not do so before you had learned your lessons. I thought you must realize it was unavoidable that I should overhear you, for you were at no pains to lower your voices. There must be no further thought of visiting this clairvoyant, whoever she may be. Think of the folly of it. You know your past, — perhaps even better than this seer," she urged, smiling. "And the future? No one knows it. If it is to be bright, we can wait for it; if gloomy, it is merciful we do not know it beforehand: we learn it only too soon. As for the women you cited, it would have been better for them had they not been warned of the fate in store for them. Don't you think Madame de Pompadour's belief in the prophecy tended to precipitate its fulfilment?"

"Perhaps," they allowed.

"I shall not ask you to promise not to go there. I know I may rely upon you. Goodnight," she murmured, turning to take the card a maid presented to her. A slight frown marred the smoothness of her brow as she read Kendall's name.

Gregory Kendall was a far distant connection

of Miss Eastlake, so he was at liberty to see Loys as often as she would permit.

Loys ran up to her room to make some slight changes in her toilet.

"You are looking tired, Loys," she exclaimed, making a *moue* at herself in the mirror, as she fastened a red rose in her hair and tried to pinch some color into her cheeks, "and it is not becoming to look tired."

She was a woman who would have taken exquisite pains with herself had she lived alone in a desert. With her, cleanliness ranked far above godliness.

She was not altogether pleased to see Kendall that night, for some unperformed duties weighed heavily upon her.

"You may stay only an hour," she said. "Probably you will wish to go long before the end of it, for I am touched with the universal discontent to-night."

"No wonder. You have been imprisoned all day. Come for a walk or a ride on the dummy."

She shook her head. "You do not know how much I have to do. Was it not Socrates who said leisure was the fairest of all possessions?"

"I don't know," he returned, moodily.

"It sounds Socratic. Well, I wish I had leisure. What do you want?" she demanded, bending toward him as if devoured by curiosity.

"A million," he answered, laconically.

"I am afraid," she sighed, "that that is everybody's ambition, or that I know a most mundane set. Yes, it must be pleasant to have a healthy bank account. Think of what money can do. It could buy me leisure, to study and to write. If I were rich, I should be kind to young girls. There are so many ways in which one could be kind without laying them under a sense of obligation. There are tickets for concerts and theatres, and gloves and flowers and pretty handkerchiefs, — you have no idea how much fine handkerchiefs cost, Gregory. The rich deserve no credit at all for being amiable; they can make so many other people happy that the pleasure must envelop even themselves. I can imagine life under given circumstances a very beautiful thing."

"And now?" he questioned.

"And now I should be glad to have done with it all. If I could clasp death, with all its mystery to me now, by putting forth my hand,

I should reach for it. Yes, I should like to go in search of the great ' Perhaps.' "

" Hush," he commanded, taking in his own her outstretched hand. " You blaspheme."

" Do I? " she demanded, wonderingly. " Death to me is a promise of peace. To you, you who believe so firmly in that heaven of yours, I should think my wish would seem only youthful impatience to arrive at the goal."

" Are you any the happier for disbelieving in heaven? You would be more content if you did not fill your mind with Spinoza, Tyndall, Weis — "

" They do not make me discontented. There is nothing beautiful to me in your idea of heaven, — it is too earthy. Why should I not read the books I like? I disbelieved what you believe long before I read, and I have always demanded the right to think for myself. I prefer to pay the toll and get out on thought's highway; I can't vegetate in blind faith. And so you do not wish to go to heaven yet a while?" she persisted, gravely.

" No."

" Ah, I have noticed that those who believe most firmly in it, object most strenuously to going there. For myself, I hope to go before

old age overtakes me. I always thought
Mohammed's dictum, that old women were to
be excluded from Paradise, a wise one, only he
modified it by saying they would first be made
young again. My eyes are already beginning
to wear out. You cannot imagine how much
they trouble me to-night."

"You use them too much," he frowned.
" But they look well."

"I know, but they burn," she murmured,
pressing her fingers upon her heavily fringed
lids. "I suppose the day will yet come when I
shall adorn a corner of Kearny Street, a shade
over my eyes and a placard on my breast:
' Please bestow a glance and a nickle on one
who can bestow neither.' I wonder, would I
have many pence given me?"

"You would if you let your eyes speak for
you," Kendall could not refrain from saying.
Loys certainly could coax compliments from
one unawares.

" So you won your Company's suit. You do
not know how proud I am of your success."

" Really, Loys?" he began, his face bright-
ening with pleasure. "I did not think you
would care or — "

"Of course I care," she hurried on. " I

like to know the successful of the land. Will
you come to see me when I am forty and still
only a teacher and you are a famous lawyer?"

"What do I care for success without you —"

She laughed nervously as she broke in: "It
is strange we two should be peering into the
future when I just reprimanded some one for
speaking of a certain Mrs. Wills who solves the
riddle of life for so much an hour. Why do we
wish to pierce the veil? Generally the future
is only, as the French have it, 'a black-bird
painted white.'"

"Do even the school-girls speak of Mrs.
Wills?" he queried. "Dr. Haswell and Dr.
Wheaton are intensely interested in her. She
lives in the same block that I do, — you know
that Queen Anne cottage set back in a garden,
— and you would be astonished to see whom
she numbers among her clients. Wheaton
mentioned her apropos of some of Yorke's
experiences in India. By the way, did I tell
you that Yorke and Van Arsdale go to Alaska
to-morrow?"

"I should like to belong to your club, too.
You meet men of brain and wit there, and the
club always entertains the well-known people
who come here. It can't help but do a man

good to rub up against bright minds — the
friction will sometimes even bring a spark or
two from us."

" That means that I am not — "

" A sorcerer," she completed, rising. " Now
you must go."

He rose regretfully. " Must I? Before I
go, promise me you will not use your eyes any
more to-night."

" Don't trouble about me. You know I
would not about you even if you were blind."

" In that case you would persuade yourself
you had always cared for me, and offer to
become my life-long nurse. Some day I shall
make believe I am ill and poor, and so get you
to consent — Oh, love, think how happy we
would be in the little home you would furnish
to your liking ! You would have time to write,
and I should not ask much of you. Only give
me the right to care for you."

She moved her hands restlessly in his grasp.
" You promised you would not bring up the old
subject again, and the very next time you come,
it all begins anew. We must give up our
attempt at friendship since you will not be content to have me for a friend ; and I cannot be
more. You must not come — "

He caught her in his arms and kissed her warm red lips. A moment later, he set her free.

"Go," she breathed. "You, too, must now realize we can continue this no longer."

He did not trust himself to speak.

She left his note of apology unanswered, and refused to see him when he called. But she missed him in the days which followed. She had sometimes looked upon his frequent comings with resentment; but they had been a break in the monotony of her life, and without him and his admiration of her, and his gossip of men in whose work she was interested, her days seemed more insipid than before.

On the following Saturday afternoon she chanced to pay a call in the same street as that in which Kendall lodged. On the way home, she paused before an old-fashioned garden, her eyes held by the wealth of pansies and roses and heliotropes abloom in sweet confusion.

"I should like the people who live here," she decided. She glanced at the house: it was a white Queen Anne cottage. Without giving herself time to think, she opened the iron gate.

She had recognized the house as that of Mrs.

Wills, and had been overcome by a desire to meet the woman. Like Laura Yorke, she thought it might be interesting as an experience. If she told her anything of the future — Well, if it were not to be a bright one, it would be beneficial to have done with hope, and if it —

"Is Mrs. Wills at home?" Loys asked, bowing to the woman who answered her ring.

"Yes, but — Did you wish to see her in regard to a reading? I am sorry, but my daughter does not read on Saturday. Her work is taxing, and she needs the two days of rest."

Loys turned away, disappointed. She liked the woman's cultured voice, and the arrangement of the hall, of which she caught a fleeting glimpse, pleased her artistic tastes. She would have liked to penetrate further.

"I am sorry to have disturbed you needlessly," she murmured.

"Would you care to make an appointment for the coming week?"

"It is impossible for me to come except on a Saturday."

The old lady opened the door further. "Perhaps my daughter will give you a sitting, anyway. Your face interests me, and I am sure it will interest her."

She ushered Loys into a cosey sitting-room, which was unoccupied, and left her alone. Loys looked about her curiously.

"Suppose Kate Tisdall or Laura Yorke should see me now," she thought, in alarm, but still in gleeful enjoyment of her position, "or Miss Eastlake!"

She had barely time to compose her face when Mrs. Wills, a stately woman of some thirty-five years, entered the room.

"I am afraid," faltered Loys, "that I had no right to intrude upon your well-deserved leisure, but your mother — "

"Yes, mother told me. I inherit my gift from her, and she is much interested in you. Will you sit here?" she proceeded, motioning to a small table and taking her seat opposite Loys. "Remove your gloves, please, and lay your hands in mine, palms downward. You are a sceptic, I see."

"But willing to be convinced," smiled Loys.

"That is broad, even for this century of progression," commented Mrs. Wills. "I may be able to see for you, perhaps not; the influences may be unfavorable. As I am a pantheist, you will understand I claim nothing phenomenal for my gift, which is cultivated; I believe every one possesses this psychometrical power in a degree. If I close my eyes, it is only that my thoughts may not be diverted: I wish to get my inner self into communication with your inner soul. Mrs. Denton (whose name, I presume, is not unfamiliar to you), if given a bit of the skeleton or the fragment of the tooth of some antedeluvian animal, saw it as it had existed. When given a bit of some article belonging to a person, she could construct from it the person, as the naturalist can build up from a bit of fossil the whole creature. I am a believer in the doctrine that what we have been makes us what we are. And now that I have completed my tedious explanation, we will proceed."

A strong current of electricity had been communicated to Loys from Mrs. Wills's hands.

"You have two sisters," observed the medium, almost at once, in a conversational tone, "both younger than you. And your mother I see quite plainly, too. Care-worn and thin, — farm-life is so wearing, — but still with a look of you about the eyes. I hear your father calling her 'Deb—'." She paused uncertainly, then added, "Deborah, is it not?"

"Yes," breathed the girl.

"Your father has been dead these twenty years. His name begins with a J—"

"No," broke in Loys, "my father is still alive."

Mrs. Wills's brow contracted. "Then who is this man who passed away many years ago, whose name began with a J, J—? It escapes me."

The woman pondered for a moment, then dropped Loys's hands.

"I am sorry, but I can do nothing for you to-day. I should have told you your father's name and your own, by this time, without error. There will be no charge, of course."

Loys put forth her hand impetuously.

"Will you not make me one more attempt?" she pleaded. "You have interested me deeply."

The woman yielded under the entreating eyes. She again took Loys's hands within her own, and her eyes closed.

"Who is this Andrew I see?" she murmured, after a little.

"My father," exclaimed Loys, before perceiving that the question had not been addressed to her.

"Her father," repeated Mrs. Wills. "A hard, cold man, and yet not so hard that he did not once forgive a grievous wrong. You nursed him through an illness a short time ago, but he is now quite well. I see no changes on the farm for many years to come, except that your second sister will marry in December."

In the silence which ensued, the girl's breath came thick and fast. It seemed extremly probable that Laura would marry Will Harland, although there was, as yet, no formal engagement, and as Mrs. Wills formed her sentences, Loys listened intently for what she would say touching her own future. She felt impelled to wrest her hands free, but was powerless to move. What folly it was to fear this — guess-work !

"Loys," recommenced the woman, hesitatingly, although the girl started at the sound of her own name on the stranger's lips, "Loys, are you going to marry this man who has been wanting you so long? What a hard little toiler you are, child, and always with the brain. The teaching has grown wearisome lately. But do not attempt another book now, when it would

mean night-work. Take care of your eyes and
you have nothing to fear, but do not abuse
them. Yet the book would be a success, — the
first was written when you were too young.
What do the two ways to Europe mean, and
both come so soon? You are going to Europe
within two months, but I am afraid it is with
the wrong one."

Then she looked off over the years, Loys
leaning still further forward ; but what the woman
said would interest only Loys.

"And the man named J——, he is so near,
yet so indistinct," murmured Mrs. Wills, opening her eyes. "Have I told you the truth?"
she asked, looking into the girl's distended eyes.

"There were some things which were true
and some I wish would come true, but do not
believe will, and some— But they are a long
way off. I shall not let the thought of them
trouble me now."

"That is right. I may, too, have been mistaken about them," Mrs. Wills prompted, with
a desire to soothe her manifest excitement.
"As a usual thing I remember nothing of what
I have seen, — my thoughts crowd, my glimpse
is so fleeting, — but I wish to caution you against
some one who is withholding something from

you, something it is of vital importance you should know."

Loys smiled with cheerful incredulity. The few people who came at all into her life she knew she could trust until death.

"You have prophesied success for me, and you have promised me a trip to Europe within two months, which is as unlikely as — "

Mrs. Wills smiled.

"What confidence you have in yourself!" whispered Loys. "You do not know what else you said. But it is a long way off; I will not think of it."

"Do you regret that you came? Oh, I am sorry if I have — "

"No, I am not sorry I came," interrupted Loys; but she shuddered as if grown suddenly cold.

Chapter V.

MISS EASTLAKE'S institute was an imposing structure, which haughtily reared its head, in prim, starched-like respectability of mien, tall and narrow, dark and stern (not unlike Miss Eastlake herself), far above the surrounding buildings. To Loys Yerrington, the round, stained-glass window in the front of the edifice always seemed to frown darkly down upon her in grim disapproval, as Miss Eastlake had a habit of doing when thwarted.

Loys's room was on the highest floor, on the corner. In the evening, when she was at length free, she would draw her low chair to the window and look out over the encircling roofs to the bay in the distance, and dream impossible dreams.

That night her dreams were not pleasant ones.

She had turned the light down until it was the merest glimmer, for her head was throbbing madly and her eyes burned.

5

"I suppose I should go to bed," she meditated doubtfully. "But it seems such a waste of time when I have so much to do. Dr. Parker said I must not use my eyes at night, nor any more than possible during the day. Yet what am I to do if I may not read at night?"

She took up a letter bearing the imprint of a well-known publishing house, which she had perused more than once that day, and read again : —

"We have read with very lively interest your novel, 'The Reverse Side,' and beg you to believe that we are by no means blind to its many and obvious excellences of both substance and form, although we must regretfully conclude that we shall be unable to add it to our list. We do not publish so much fiction as some houses, and trust you will readily find some other publishers more confident than we can quite bring ourselves to be that your book will meet the difficult conditions of successful novel publication, at present. We return the MS. by express, and hope you will accept our sincere thanks for the opportunity of considering it."

"The book must have merit, or they would not write me such a letter," Loys declared, "but

I can see its faults now. If I had only the time
to write the plot I have in mind ! I am more
mature now. I began to write that book when
I was twenty-two, and it has been to four firms.
Each one keeps it about three months, and two
weeks are consumed in its forwarding to New
York and return. What a disadvantage we
labor under here, away from all literary or musical atmosphere, — from every art-center. In
less than a fortnight vacation will be here, and
I shall go to the farm. But there will be no
time for writing there, for Laura will wish me to
help her with her trousseau. I hate the thought
of going : I am ashamed of it, but I cannot
overcome it. How can Laura love Will Harland? He is so odiously funny and petty.
And he drinks, — she knows he does, and that
his father was a dipsomaniac. Oh, she has no
right to marry him and entail such misery on
her children. I wonder if she really loves him,
or whether it is only the desire to escape from
the hard ugliness of her life and to have a home
of her own which prompts her to marry him.

" It is always an alluring thought to a woman,
— that of having a home of her own," she
continued. " I know I should assume such
matronly airs if I were the mistress of a six-

roomed house, and order my little servant
about simply to feel a delightful sense of authority.   And in the evening, when he came home,
and we sat down to our dainty table — "

She levelled her cottage-building to the ground
with a harsh laugh, and raised the gas defiantly.
The words " Chapter IV " stared up at her from
the note-book she opened.   She had begun the
story a few days after her interview with Mrs.
Wills.   She had no faith in the prophecy that
she would shortly go to Europe, but she believed success might be hers if she could but
find the time to write another book.   She had
disregarded the advice not to tax her eyes, and
had been forced to go to the oculist.   For the
past few days she had adhered to his directions,
but the story had been continuously in her
thoughts, and now the words trembled at the
nib of her pen, and hurriedly dissolved themselves into ink.

Two pages were soon covered, and then the
lines began to dance before her eyes.   She set her
lips firmly and commenced the third, but soon
it was all a hopeless blur.   The pen fell from
her nerveless fingers, and she again turned low
the lights as if to hide from herself her blinding
tears.   She caught her quivering lip between

her sharp, white teeth, to choke back the heavy sobs which threatened to suffocate her. She must not cry, she would not cry, when she knew tears would injure her eyes.

Some one rapped at the door.

" What is it, Jane ? " she asked.

The maid handed her Kendall's card. Across its face he had written, " Do not refuse to see me. I have come only to bid you good-by."

She hesitated momentarily, then left the room. It would be well to escape her rabid thoughts for a time.

As she entered the apartment in which Kendall awaited her, she involuntarily covered her eyes to shield them from the glare of the lights. Kendall paled at the action, then quickly extinguished two of the gas jets and lowered the third.

" Have you been caring for your eyes ? " he demanded. " Are they better ? "

She looked at him in cold wonderment. " How did you know they have been troubling me ? "

" I saw you go into Parker's office, and when you came out you looked so frightened that I went in myself," he explained, with simple directness. "Dr. Parker is an old friend of mine."

"You had no right — "

"No, I know; but I could not help myself."

He looked so humble, so conscious of his wrong-doing, that Loys felt a mad inclination to laugh, for generally Kendall wore a rather self-satisfied, autocratic air.

"Have you been ill?" she queried, in quick self-reproach, as she noticed his wan face and dejected attitude.

"No. Loys, Loys, what heavy punishment you can mete out without a qualm!"

"It was a wise decree, and if you persist you will make me regret having seen you. If you only make an effort you can displace me from your heart, and after a little some pretty, young girl will enter your life, who will love you entirely, and whom you will — "

"Don't. It hurts me to see you placidly arranging my marriage to another. If I should ever hear of your marriage — " His face set in an expression of cruel, malignant hatred. "So Laura is going to marry Will Harland," he proceeded. "Are you glad?"

"Why should I pretend to be glad to you?" she demurred. "I think him altogether un-

worthy of Laura — you do not know how unselfish she is. She loves him, but, oh, she has no
right to marry him. We who have always known
him are aware he drinks, and that it is an in-
herited weakness. Last summer, when I saw
how matters were tending, I did my utmost to
open her eyes to the wrong she would be doing,
but she would not listen. If she would be harming only herself, I should have said no word ;
but she has no right to perpetuate misery. It
is criminal."

"Suppose you loved Will Harland, with a
love which filled your whole being, would you
not marry him?" He watched her with covert
eagerness.

"No, I would not. I would rather die ten
thousand deaths than marry such a man," she
declared, with quiet firmness.

"You do not know what you would do," he
broke forth, fiercely.

The girl was too weary to carry the discus-
sion farther. With partially closed eyes, she
leaned against the cushions and watched him
idly as he clutched at the inoffending tassel of
his arm-chair.

"He is looking especially handsome and
well-groomed to-night," she meditated. "It

would be well for Gregory if he could have a new suit every day in the week. His clothes lose their first freshness so soon. I believe he leaves them in an unsightly mass on the floor, as they fall from him. It is strange he should be so careless in that regard, for his linen is always immaculate, and he is more than particular about his person. Yet I have seen him wear clothes sadly in need of a brushing; and it is easier to forgive a spot on a man's character than one on his clothes. It seems to me I see a great deal too much," she deplored. "It is a mistake to know people too intimately. I always admired Dante more before I learned that he sometimes did not change his linen for weeks."

"Tell me something about the condition of your eyes," he urged. "Have you been obeying Parker's instructions?"

"I cannot do otherwise. They refuse to permit me to work."

"Do you wish me to read to you now? And all this week is at your disposal."

In her tired state his kindness touched her inexpressibly. "You are too kind to me, dear old Greg," she whispered, tremulously.

It comforted her to have him with her.

" What are you going to do with your evenings?" he asked.

" Every one has been more than good, and has offered to read or write for me, but — "

"You never did like any one to read to you. Poor little girl," he murmured, under his breath.

" Don't remind me of unpleasant things," she cautioned, trying to speak lightly. "At least I am rich in one very good friend."

" I want you to listen to what I am going to say now as coming simply from your friend. Let me speak on to the end, once and for all. As I told you, I have seen Parker, and he says you must never again abuse your eyes as you have in the past. If you cannot work for yourself at night, I know how unhappy you will be. Can you not persuade yourself that you like me enough to give yourself into my keeping? I should try not to fret you by my love. You would have time for your studies and work, and to arrange and rearrange your hair — how many times a day do you wish to do it? And there would be your light household duties, and time enough to be womanly, as you phrase it. Do you — "

" I cannot let you go on," she moaned, interlacing her fingers.

"And you would teach the cook all your famous recipes," he went on, unheeding her interruption, although his fingers closed still more savagely about the tassel. "What a pretty home it would be, with all the modest little articles of *vertu* we should accumulate in Europe!" he concluded, playing his last card.

"Are you going to Europe?" she cried.

"Did I forget to tell you?" he asked, with cunning hypocrisy. "It is about the affairs of the Williams estate that I am going. I leave in ten days, and shall be away three months. Not a long while, but there will be time to see something of the Old World."

"How glad I am you are going, and how I shall miss you, dear old Greg!" She realized the truth of her words. The city would seem bleak and desolate without him. It was true she had not seen him within the past month, but she knew he was within reach.

"Why should you be sorry to see the last of an ogre?" he said, with a sad smile. "You will be about going to the farm, and in the festive time of Laura's wedding you will not devote a single thought to me. You know, Will Harland and his followers always make a merry time for themselves."

She repressed a shudder. The thought of going to the farm and meeting Will Harland and his friends weighed upon her remorselessly.

"I suppose I must not detain you longer," he added.

With a dim sense of pain she watched him rise. How powerful and strong he looked, and how weak and weary she felt.

His subtle instincts told him that a word too much or a word too little would make or mar his life's happiness. His nerves were strung to the utmost tension, though he was outwardly collected. Never before had he been so alert to her needs as that night.

He knelt down and stole his arm about her, saying, softly, "Can't you decide to make me happy, Loys?"

She felt his arm, but she was so weary that she was glad of it. Suddenly she sat erect, pushing him away. The moment was pregnant with importance to them both.

"Wait," she breathed, her face feverishly aglow. "Let me be honest with you and show you my true self. It is the thought of seeing Europe which is bribing me, and the fact that I shall have time to write. If it were not for that, I should not —"

"I know, sweet," the man interrupted, in mad triumph.

"Suppose that afterward there should come into my life a man — "

He crushed her to him in quick fright. "There will be none such," he affirmed, jealously.

"We have known each other so long there is no danger that we are being deceived. Even under existing circumstances, you are sure you want me?" she asked, with a pretence at grave humility.

He drew her hands to his mouth and kissed them passionately. "Don't you know what you are to me?" he whispered, hoarsely.

She bent down and put her arms about his neck, faltering, "I will try to make you happy. At least you shall never regret marrying me, dear."

He was careful to alarm her by no outburst of feeling. He realized that he must restrain himself at all hazards ; and she thought it restful to give in and be cared for.

With his keen perception of what was best for his interests, Kendall, before leaving, informed Miss Eastlake of Loys's promise. The marriage was set for noon of the tenth day from that evening, when they would depart at once for the East.

"I wish your father were here," Loys said. "I know he will be glad; he always said he loved me as a daughter."

"We shall see him in London," Kendall answered. "All my intimate friends are away. Van Arsdale and Yorke have not yet returned from Alaska, and Penelope Browning wrote me to-day that she does not expect to be here for another fortnight."

When he finally left her, and Miss Eastlake, too, had ceased to murmur her regret at losing her, Loys went to her room.

"And so I am to be Gregory's wife after all," she reflected, as she sat down in the old familiar attitude. "When I sat here a short while ago, furnishing the little home, he did not sit opposite me at table, but neither do I know who did. And love — I believe it exists only in novels," she asseverated, "so why should I alarm myself over a phantom, the best definition of which I ever read was, 'Nothing, of which one is afraid.' When I think of the married people I know, I cannot fasten upon one who is more in love than I am, perhaps, with Gregory. They all seem to bear each other a decorous, proper affection. We leave it to dear unselfish Gregory to be so foolish as to think more of another than of himself. Perhaps I am too self-centered to be capable of an absorbing passion. No, I am not afraid of the consequences of the step I have taken."

She repeated the thought many times in different form, as if to reassure herself.

"Love is so often a fictitious emotion," she pursued, "and yet I wish I cared more for him. But every one is agreed that sincere liking endures better than love, so I need not fear," she concluded, as she imprudently began to write to her father and mother.

The reiteration had dulled her senses. She was determined to close her eyes to the fact that she had reared a house of cards whose foundation rested not on love.

"Oh, the little more, and how much it is !
And the little less, and what worlds away !"

Chapter VI.

LOYS never cared to look back upon the trip to Europe.

In the short time which had intervened between her engagement and marriage, Kendall had been wise enough not to demand much of her. His delicacy had endeared him to her, but the last vestige of his consideration vanished when he found she was indissolubly his. He forgot his promise of patience with her until she loved him. He remembered nothing but that she was now his wife, and she smiled in mordant mockery of her confidence in his vain promises, and told herself she must not forget he was her husband. There was, however, small danger of his permitting her to forget it.

If he had been content to keep his love more hidden, it is possible Loys might have grown to love him; but he was too completely overwhelmed by his success in having won her to temper his attentions with nice discretion.

To have shown him, by the smallest sign, that his neglect of the conditions of his bond fretted her, would have been to recall to him that she had sold herself, and that he was untrue to the spirit of the barter. In a measure, she had forfeited her own self-esteem by the transaction, and she was unwilling to recall it to his mind.

The run through Europe always seemed to Loys, afterward, a hideous nightmare, broken by some few hours of happiness. Kendall appeared to be imbued with a desire to see things simply to say he had seen them, and Loys, an unwilling victim, was mercilessly dragged hither and thither, and hurried off again after a tantalizing vision of what it had been her life-long dream to study. At first she offered a spirited resistance, and Kendall accommodated himself to her promptings. But her enthusiasm was stultified by his lack of appreciation and evident boredom; and as she grew to recognize more thoroughly their unshared tastes, she assumed, with indifferent success, a stoical ignoring of her own wishes and fitted hers to his. She was benumbed with pain when she allowed herself to linger on the disappointment of the trip, and the thought of what it might have been.

In London they met Kendall's father, with
whom Loys had always been a great favorite.
He could not do enough for her ; but he treated
his son coldly, and while with him, Gregory
was ill at ease and surly.

It was at Paris on the fourth day before their
return to America that Loys first met Penelope
Browning.   Loys was alone when Penelope's
card was brought to her.   Scarcely had she signified her readiness to receive her visitor than
Kendall appeared.

" We shall be detained somewhat," Loys
remarked.   " Your friend, Miss Browning, is
here."

" Where is the servant?   Tell him that we
are not at home," directed Kendall, excitedly.

It was too late — Penelope was even then on
the threshold, and he turned to greet her
graciously.

" My being here is another proof of my
good-nature," averred Penelope, as she still
held Loys's hand.   " It is not an easy task to
forgive one who has caused so great a disappointment as you gave me.   Now that I see
you, I can scarcely forgive you."

Loys regarded her in open-eyed amazement.

6

"Tell us how you discovered that we were here," broke in Kendall.

"I had a letter from Riker Van Arsdale. An all-consuming curiosity to meet you," she went on, turning to Loys, "impelled my visit the moment I learned your hotel. You know it must always remain an enigma to me why you preferred Gregory's chaperonage to mine."

"I am afraid I am very stupid," Loys ventured, smiling in perplexed expectancy, "but I do not understand."

Kendall gnawed his mustache impatiently, but made no endeavor to explain matters.

"I believe," began Penelope, laughing softly, "that you are afraid of my just anger. Ah, you should have seen me when I received Gregory's note, saying you thanked me for the invitation, but preferred seeing Europe under his auspices."

Before the completion of the sentence, a sickening suspicion overcame Loys. She darted one quick, comprehensive glance at her husband's disturbed face, and then a fixed, wooden smile settled itself upon her mouth. Afterward she flattered herself that she had acted well, but she did not impose upon the woman opposite

her, who would have given much to be able
to recall her words.

"I shall always blame Riker Van Arsdale for
not having given me a suggestion as to the
unwarrantable insolence of my desires," Penelope continued, flowingly.

"And was the choice I made a wise one?"
asked Loys, placing her hand on Kendall's
chair, with a caressing smile.

As their eyes met, the two women knew each
other, and each cried out at the fraud which
had been practised.

Kendall's agitation subsided. He was now
glad that Penelope had called, for he had
feared the meeting and Loys's anger at his
deception. Long ago he had once seen Loys
aroused, and it was not an experience he
thought he would care to provoke again.
Everything had passed so smoothly, he was
relieved that he would no longer suffer the
suspense.

Penelope Browning looked from husband to
wife in bitter dismay.

"Some one in San Francisco spoke of this
marriage as though she had practised black art
to gain him," she meditated, "and said Gregory Kendall had thrown himself away on a poor

school-teacher.   Blind fools! could they not
see?   Why did I not go to her the night after
Laura mentioned her?"

A short while later she rose to go.

"I wish you would let me be your guide
during the remainder of your stay here,"
she entreated.   "Can you not give me to-
morrow?"

"My days will be crowded with business
affairs," Kendall declared, in reply to Loys's
questioning eyes, "but I have no doubt Loys
will be glad to be under your guardianship."

"What would Riker Van Arsdale say now?"
Penelope pondered, when Kendall had closed
the carriage door upon her.   "I know Gregory
deceived her once; I wonder if— Riker is
right: she is an interesting study.   Only I wish
I could feel that she would not prove interesting to the end,— that everything in her life
would be ordinary and commonplace.   It is
always safest so.   When she laid her hand on
his chair—"   An hysterical little laugh escaped her.

Kendall returned to the room with no mis-
givings.   An indefinable smile was upon Loys's
lips as she arranged the chrysanthemums Penelope Browning had brought her.   He stood

watching her in awkward silence for a few moments, then he hazarded : —

" Are you not going to scold me for my deception, Loys ? "

She bent her head to one side, gravely criticising her work.

" Loys, don't say you regret having married me," he cried, a sharp intonation of pain vibrating through his voice. " You don't, my love, do you ? "

" No, no, I do not regret it," she asserted, vehemently, hiding her face on his breast. " I will not regret it."

A listener would have imagined she was endeavoring to persuade herself rather than him.

" Tell me," she resumed, after a little, " had you received Miss Browning's note that night I promised to marry you ? "

" Yes. Of course I would have told you of her offer if you had not agreed to be my wife," he affirmed, with virtuous disinterest. He had already shaken from his sloping shoulders all responsibility of wrong-doing. " Afterward there was no need to mention it, was there ? "

There was a moment of passionate contempt, then she shook her head, too spent by conflict-

ing emotions to contradict him.   Already she
had learned to suffer and say nothing.

The dream of what the journey might have
been became a reality under Penelope Browning's chaperonage during the few days left
them.   They seemed to have known each other
all their life long.   There was no clashing of
tastes, no jarring of ideas, although each asserted her own rich individuality.

It was on their last afternoon in Paris that
Kendall received from Rome a congratulatory
letter . from Bishop Yorke, who apologized for
his neglect by stating that he had expected to
meet them on the continent.   He wrote that
he had sent Mrs. Kendall a ring which was
supposed to have belonged to Lucretia Borgia.
The gift arrived at the same time.   It was a
ring of Etruscan gold, of curious workmanship,
which contained five graduated turquoises, of
an exquisite blue, set horizontally.   Penelope
Browning was with Loys when it came to
hand.

"By accident, Mr. Yorke fastened upon my
favorite stone," Loys commented.   "I hope
the turquoises will not change color now that
they have come into my possession."

"I am not sure that it was an accident,"

Penelope protested, nonchalantly. " He once told me that the most becoming stone to a pretty hand is a turquoise or a black intaglio, — they bring out the whiteness of the skin. I fancy he remembered what Laura said of your hand."

"When was that?" queried Loys, flushing slightly.

"The same night she piqued my curiosity about you. You don't know what a keen admirer you have in Laura Yorke."

"How immeasurably she did look down upon me ! " Loys scoffed, laughing incredulously. " I was surprised that she saw me, — she was so far above me. I envied Laura Yorke her feeling of calm superiority over the rank and file, — it was an impregnable armor. But I understand her brother is not at all like her."

"I wish you had met him," murmured Penelope Browning.

❦

Chapter VII

LOYS had not overestimated to herself the charm she would find in a home of her own.

Upon their return, Kendall had built for her, on the heights of the city, an unconventional house which had about it a strong air of individuality, — the result of Loys's frequent consultations with the architect. To the furnishing of the house she devoted her best endeavors; but when it was completed and they took possession of it on that first night, Kendall's approbation more than recompensed her. It was no longer a house : it was a home.

Her household seemed to run itself, and Loys insisted that it did.

" All I do is to go round each morning with my little can, to oil up the screws and joints of the machinery," she explained to Kendall and Van Arsdale, one evening at dinner. " Don't imagine I deserve any particular credit: any woman who is not a fool can manage her household well, without much expense of time or trouble. I am only careful not to let you see me with the oil-can in my hand and not to seem weighted down with my cares. I was fortunate, too, in securing Mary at the start. When she came to us, nearly everything but a potato in its overcoat was an unknown quantity to her. But now she duplicates every *plat* known to me with far greater skill than I can master, and you know I claim to be a culinary genius. It is my one natural talent. Every month I say shamefacedly, 'She must not stay any longer; any one would be glad to give her twice what we pay.' It must be quite three months since Mary and I began that pleasant little illusion, and still I make no violent effort to make her go, and she makes none either. I must arouse myself soon, however, and, taking my courage in my hands, send her away."

When Van Arsdale first commenced to frequent the house, Loys was not altogether at her ease with him. She feared she bored him, for his face rarely relaxed into a look of interest ; but when she discovered that he called upon no other woman, and came to her as often as twice a week, and sent her books and papers

he had marked, she ceased to doubt his liking
for her.

They were mutually attracted intellectually;
but she told him, after a while, as well as
Kendall, the happenings of her day, her household experiences, and her trials and failures.
She never forgot, or allowed any one to forget,
that she was primarily a woman.

She fostered Kendall's ambition, and made
him proud enough of her good opinion to seek
to win it; and when he saw his own progress
and the stride forward he had made in the
minds of those whose views he respected, he
felt proud of himself, as well as of his wife,
whose influence he recognized.

She loved peace, but believed it can be pur-
chased at too high a price; she was, however,
at all times tactful. When she won Kendall
over, she wore no conscious air of triumph, and
when she yielded, she did so unconditionally
and gracefully. His friends remarked Kendall's
improvement; and he had improved, for Loys
had not hesitated to correct those faults it was
possible to mention to him, without wounding
him unutterably, as she expected him to correct her.

She had not deceived herself in regard to

her literary work. Upon returning from Europe,
she continued her novel, and brought it to completion within four months. Riker Van Arsdale aided her much by his criticism, for she
read the manuscript to him and Kendall before
sending it to be typewritten. It was immediately accepted by one of the foremost houses
of New York, and, upon its appearance, proved
to be one of the successes of the year.

And yet, somehow, her success left her dis-
satisfied and cold. She now possessed the one
thing she had thought essential to her happiness, — success. It may have been that this
tingling wine had been too long kept in view,
and that she had overestimated its qualities, or
perhaps it had been too long in the pouring
out and the air had reached it; for when the
glass was held to her lips, the wine was flat.
It had all seemed so much better in anticipation that she wondered dully if it could have
been for this tepid feeling of gratification that
she had so striven and hungered.

Penelope Browning had returned shortly
before the appearance of the novel, and again
taken up her abode in her magnificent residence just a block or two from the Kendall's.
The intimacy had been kept warm by numerous

letters, and Penelope quickly insinuated herself
into the sunniest compartments of Loys's affec-
tions.

Penelope took as much satisfaction in Loys's
success as if she herself had written the book,
and was inclined to quarrel with Loys on
account of her apathetic acceptance of her
good-fortune.

Two or three months after the appearance of
the book there came to Loys the greatest happiness which can befall a woman. She jealously
guarded the trembling hope to herself for a
short time, but finally told Kendall. She was
thrown back upon herself by his manner of
receiving the intelligence; but not even his lack
of warmth, his jealousy at the thought of divid-
ing her love with another, could lessen her
quiet joy. Penelope Browning's words seemed
cold and forced to Loys, but they did not
wound her. She was already transfigured by
her coming glory, and felt only a vague pity
for Kendall and Penelope, because they could
not fully enter into her great happiness.

Kendall's temper was nervous and uneven
about that time, but Loys never once was impa-
tient. Nothing seemed to fret or disturb her;
but in the early part of May she began to long

for the country, and as Kendall was called East
at that moment on important business, she
accepted Penelope's invitation to spend the
summer quietly with her in her cottage at Ross
Valley. They did no entertaining whatever,
yet to both the summer slipped away only too
rapidly.

In the latter part of August they returned to
the city, and Loys seemed to miss the long
days spent in the open air; but she made no
murmur, even to her mother, who was making
her a visit of indefinite length.

Loys had been so brave and patient all along,
and so free from fear, that she had imbued
those around her with her spirit; but in September they almost lost her, as well as the child,
whose life was sacrificed for the mother's.

She regained her strength slowly; there seemed
an utter want of desire to live. There was no
battling with her grief or weariness. Death
appeared to her a blessed relief; but when at
length she found that it does not come because
of the wishing, and her tired brain realized the
agony she was causing those who loved her,
she shook off her lethargy. Little by little she
resumed her duties, and strove with fine courage
to forget the ordeal she had undergone. Not

even to Kendall did she ever refer to her sorrow. She could not forget that he had failed to rejoice with her, and she endeavored to rid herself of the impression that both he and Penelope, as well as Kendall's father, had been relieved that the child had not lived.

Her physician, Dr. Haswell, who took a strong interest in her, wished her to go out; but at first she found it impossible to do so. Then Kendall began to evince a desire for society; but neither he nor Penelope Browning would go without her, and Loys, who could fathom their suddenly conceived tastes, threw aside her distaste for meeting people, and began to frequent the world once again.

Chapter VIII.

ꝑENELOPE BROWNING had entertained at dinner that evening a party
of fourteen. There were originally to have
been sixteen, but during the afternoon Kendall had telephoned her that Loys was not well,
and he wished Penelope would tell her she
was not to make the effort of attending the
dinner.

Penelope had smothered her discomfiture
and followed out his instructions, professing
a great surprise at seeing Loys extended on
the couch.

"You are not to dream of making the effort
of sitting so long at table," she had good-
naturedly said, "but manage to come at ten for
an hour or two. I wish you were not feeling
ill. I intended you to go in to dinner with
Bishop Yorke. I am very anxious to have you
meet Bishop and the Lidderdales."

The coffee had been served in the drawing-
room, and Penelope had cast many a glance

in the direction of the door before Loys and
Kendall made their appearance.

"I began to think you had deserted me,"
exclaimed Penelope, as she advanced to meet
them.

"I am not sure that I was wise to bring
Loys," returned Kendall, regarding his wife
with anxious eyes.

"We are attracting every one's attention,"
demurred Loys. "I am only a trifle fagged
from mounting the steps. May I sit next to
Mr. Van Arsdale until I recover myself?"

They certainly had drawn the attention of
the company to themselves. Kendall had
grown somewhat stouter in the two years of
his marriage, but he was still a very handsome
man, and as he crossed the room to welcome
Bishop Yorke, his face was illumined by a smile
of pleasure, which made one instinctively feel
his good-nature.

Loys had always had an individual charm.
She was an interesting-looking woman, rather
than a strictly handsome one, and that night
she was looking remarkably striking. The
other women present were all in light-colored
gowns, but Loys wore a gown of some sheer
black material, which was slightly open at the

throat.   A bunch of violets drooped at her breast.

" Do you know," she began to Van Arsdale, " when I came in I felt every separate eye in the room upon me."

" You looked unabashed by the gaze of the select public."

" Happily, the cunning of a blush is, with me, to be numbered among the lost arts. Again, I felt I could bear the most rigorous criticism.   I am iron-clad in the knowledge that I indulged myself in a leisurely toilet, and that the mirror was kind to me to-night," she confessed, with bare-faced assurance.

" Be more guarded.   What would you say if I should tell you that a piece of soot embellished your nose ? "

" Merely that you were exercising a luxuriant imagination," she returned, with exasperating serenity.   " I scrutinized myself before entering."

" It must be delightfully comfortable to be so satisfied with one's self," sighed Van Arsdale.

" It is, and so novel.   I have come to the conclusion that it does not do to be too honest with one's self.   Of course the tall, exceedingly

7

well-groomed looking man upon whom Gregory
is beaming is Mr. Yorke."

"Yes. You will be glad to learn he is going
to make this his resting-place for a while. His
affairs here need attention. I imagine you two
will be great friends."

"I know what it will mean for you to have
him. I do not know that I believe in luck, but
life is certainly made easier for some people
than for others, and it has been made easy for
Mr. Yorke, hasn't it? I never knew until
to-night that he was a lawyer and at one time
connected with Mr. Warner."

"His association with Warner lasted little
over a year, and then because of his skill with
his pen and brush he drifted into his connection
with the magazine people. It was Warner's
fault."

"Why?"

"Yorke was young and enthusiastic, and
beneath Warner's successful methods he did
not know he would find such unscrupulousness
countenanced under the name of business. He
had long had a strong dislike for Warner, and
one morning, when every clerk in the office was
wishing he would win in the lottery or suddenly
fall heir to a modest competency, that he might

quit Warner's employ, Yorke, being rich enough to indulge himself in the luxury of retaining his own self-respect, walked in upon Warner and announced his intention of withdrawing from the firm."

"Tell me what had happened," Loys commanded.

" It was something in this wise," Van Arsdale kindly proceeded, noting that her breath was still coming and going too quickly. "One of the junior clerks, who occupied the same office with Warner, inadvertently hung his topcoat on Warner's rack, and Warner took the fire-tongs, placed the coat upon them, and carried them out into the office."

"What! Yet I suppose Mr. Warner considers himself a gentleman."

"No, I think not. Warner is really too bright a man to so delude himself," maintained Van Arsdale, dryly.

At that moment Penelope broke in upon them with Yorke.

"What have you two been speaking of so earnestly?" she demanded, after presenting Yorke to Loys.

"Do not ask," kindly prompted Yorke. "Can you not see from Riker's self-conscious air that he has been speaking of us, and not all good?"

"What a comfortable possession is an easy conscience!" laughed Loys. "Here you are, Penelope, wondering whether we can have discovered and been discussing your latest indiscretion, while I should have been perfectly at ease if you had been speaking of me, safe in the knowledge there is no evil to be whispered of me."

"And I too," chimed in Van Arsdale.

"I am afraid that if you were to come out in your true colors, you would go round in a yellow cover, like the French novels," Yorke averred.

Penelope and Van Arsdale wandered away.

"Do you know that you caused me a great disappointment by your default?" Yorke continued, still standing. "Penelope had promised me your company at dinner."

Loys laid her hand upon the chair beside her own, and smiled up at him.

"Probably we would be more comfortable if I were seated," he agreed, smiling in turn. "I too often forget my inconvenient length. I shall impress you with the idea that I should be more at ease if I took a seat upon the mantel; these low chairs were never meant for a man of my size."

"And so you have concluded to sit upon your own hearth-rug and purr," she ventured.

"Yes. It seems my affairs require supervision, and I am not grieving that I am no longer to be like Noah's dove, lighting here and there, only to be again on the wing."

"I hope you, too, come with an olive leaf in your mouth."

"Do I not look like a man with a seraphic temperament?"

"I am not prepared to hazard an opinion," she asserted, after a meditative pause, making a pretence of studying his features.

Yorke had entered life under the charter of success. From his cradle his charm had been undisputed. He could remember nothing he had wished for which had been withheld. His honors had come to him without labor; that he took the highest degree in his class, that he was considered the first stroke in his team, were nothing to his credit, his classmates protested. He had been born with a fine amount of intelligence, with a magnificent physique, and with the proverbial golden spoon in his mouth; moreover, it bore a crest. There had been times when it

had seemed that his banner might be over-
thrown, but his indomitable will and persever-
ence had won the battle. He had come to
consider success as his birthright.

"I remember dreaming once of being way-
laid by a highwayman, and his face wore the
same expression of grim determination as does
Mr. Yorke's — money or your life, it said. He
would have something. I am convinced he
never has vain wishes, only invincible wills,"
Loys mused.

"Has not my reputation preceded me?"
Yorke went on. "I had hoped Kendall or
Penelope would have told you all about me."

"Hoped?" echoed Loys, raising her level
brows. "Most of us would rather imagine we
had not been discussed beforehand."

"Perhaps the fact that Penelope and I have
been friends for more than twenty years will
attest my first statement."

"Not at all. Penelope is forgiving in the
extreme. I have never been able to entice her
into the least semblance of a quarrel. Yet I do
not plume myself upon my good-nature, nor
have I heard any one else mention it. But,"
she added, with a deprecatory sigh of comical
resignation, "I never expect to be properly

appreciated by any one but myself until I am in my grave."

"Grave?" he repeated. "I trust cremation will have become an assured fact before I die."

"Have you ever thought that they might bury you while you were still alive? I have. I am going to hang a placard upon my bed, as did Hans Andersen, 'Don't bury me ; I think I am alive.' I hope they will cremate me."

"If I get to the crematory first, I shall ask that you be appointed first stoker," put in Kendall, leaning over her.

"I am trying to convince Gregory," she pursued, unheeding her husband's frivolity, "that cremation is a much cleaner and more humane course than burial, but my efforts are greeted with but small success. I imagine Gregory believes that to speak of my demise would hasten it."

Kendall sauntered away. He had a childish objection to speaking of death.

"At least, cremation is more economical," Yorke allowed, "and Kendall could keep you on the chimney-piece in a beautiful urn, and murmur to visitors, 'There slumbers my beloved wife.' A large family need have but one good-sized urn. I wonder if on the Day

of Judgment the contents of that urn would turn
out a composite figure."

They laughed together at his conceit, and
Loys, who had been slipping her rings on and
off her fingers, at that moment dropped the
turquoise.

"Thank you," she murmured, as he restored
it to her. "Do you recognize your gift? It
was more than kind to send it to me, for you
must have had some friend who would have
welcomed it, on account of its historical associa-
tions, with as much appreciation as I."

"As soon as I saw it, I knew it was intended
for you. You see, Laura had described you to
us one night in this very house. Do you still
retain your love for Heine?"

"How did you know he was one of my favor-
ites?" she queried, in turn.

There crept into his eyes, too, an expression
of blank surprise.

"Surely," he thought, "she must be aware I
know of her admiration for the man, else why
should I have sent her that book?"

"Again my information came through Laura,"
he pursued, aloud. "She has a strong regard
for you."

Loys smothered her astonishment.

"Almost the first German work I read was 'The Book Le Grand,' which I found simple because I knew it so well in the English. I still have that battered, annotated little volume, which is so dear to me that, although I have continually determined to buy another, I never do."

He regarded her curiously, then glanced across the room at his sister, whose eyes were at that second fixed upon them.

"Loys," Penelope began, coming up to them, "Mrs. Lidderdale is very anxious to meet you. You had no right, Bishop, to monopolize Mrs. Kendall in your selfish fashion."

"I am afraid it was I who monopolized Mr. Yorke. You must not let me be so thoughtless another time," smiled Loys, turning away.

At Penelope's solicitation, the man who sat next to Laura Yorke went to the piano, and Yorke sank into the vacant place. When the song came to an end, Yorke turned to his sister, saying, "Do you remember my once giving you a work of Heine for—"

"Don't go on," the girl interrupted. "I remember all the incidents: they are unpleasantly impressed upon my memory. I tried to confess a day or two after you gave me the book,

but my courage failed me. I clumsily overturned a bottle of ink, which thoroughly satu-
rated the book. As Miss Yerrington — I mean
Mrs. Kendall — had a distaste for soiled volumes,
I made no mention of it to her, and, as I before
told you, I was afraid, at the time, of your dis-
pleasure. Are you very angry?"

A half-smile parted his lips : it was not altogether a pleasant smile, and under it Laura grew
slightly discomposed.

"I never before knew you were a coward,"
he finally observed. It was a long time since
she had seen Yorke so aroused.

"You seem to doubt my having overturned
the ink," she commented, haughtily.

He measured her with partially closed eyes,
then walked away.

She complacently arranged the roses at her
waist. Ah, it had not been so foolish, after all,
to be afraid of — Loys Yerrington.

As Loys and Kendall walked home that evening, she said, "Penelope was at her best
to-night. What were you two last laughing
about ? "

"At what do you suppose? At some remark
of her own," Kendall observed, with some
little asperity. "There is nothing more unbe-

coming a woman than cleverness; that is, unless she is clever enough to conceal it. No trait becomes more quickly offensive than the brilliancy of which a person is conscious and with which she desires to impress others. I, don't like clever women."

Loys declined to construe his statement as a reflection upon herself.

"You cannot be speaking with Penelope in mind," she protested, with rare loyalty to her friend.

Kendall had wasted upon Penelope that night two witticisms which had been capable of arousing even his own fastidious approval, and an epigram which had never before failed to make a deep impression, yet she had noticed them by only a perfunctory smile. She had been either completely absorbed in her laughter over some remark of her own, or had been waiting with visible impatience until he should finish speaking, when she intended to give utterance to one of her own carefully prepared impromptu effects, which he saw trembling upon her lips. It was, therefore, with a due appreciation of his own blessings that he felt Loys's arm within his own. Loys belonged to that almost extinct race of beings which is not

swayed by an overwhelming desire to be the
actor, — never the audience.

"Here we are at our own door. Let us
walk round the block, Gregory. It is a crime
to waste such a perfect night in sleep."

"No," he returned, resolutely, "I am not
going to encourage you in your owl-like habits.
I did not enjoy this evening so thoroughly that
I desire to prolong it."

"But I did," she asserted, wilfully, resisting
the arm he placed about her in an endeavor to
draw her over the threshold. "Take your arm
away, or the conductor and engineer on the
next passing dummy will think I am the cook
and that you are her young man."

She gazed up at the star-lit, cloudless sky,
her eyes dwelling gratefully upon the splendor
of the new-born moon.

"Of what are you thinking?" Kendall whispered, enfolding her closer.

She slipped away, laughing mischievously,
and pointed to the crescent-moon, about which
the luminous halo was vigorously marked.

"Only that though this January has been like
our usual February weather, I am afraid it
intends to rain to-morrow night, simply to give
our guests a chance to soil our new rugs."

Then she followed him into the house, vaguely wondering why she had spoken of the weather when she knew she had been thinking of Bishop Yorke. She would ask Penelope how he came by the sabre scar on his forehead. The story escaped her. She knew he had received the wound through risking his life for another, but for whom she could not think.

Penelope would know.

Chapter IX.

MRS. LUTTRELL was undeniably sleeping when Yorke was announced. The book in her lap dropped to the floor at her precipitate start.

"Is it you, Bishop?" she asked, blinking drowsily upon him. "Penelope is dining at the Kendall's to-night, but she left word that if you came early you were to join her there. I shall call for you at half-past ten, to take you to the Trotter's."

Yorke debated a moment. It was quite clear that Mrs. Luttrell was not anxious for his company; and as Loys had never invited him to call, he did not know that he cared to enter her home unasked.

"You will enjoy yourself at the Kendall's," garrulously ran on Mrs. Luttrell, "for Loys really understands what home should be. If there were more such women, we should hear less of divorce suits and marriage being a failure; but then she has rather antiquated ideas

about a wife's duties. Penelope told her that
she intended to leave word that you were to
follow her. Loys was very glad to think you
were coming."

Yorke found himself at the Kendall's door
before he had fully decided whether he was wise
to follow his inclinations in obeying Penelope's
orders.

The maid opened the door, and he stood
within the pretty hall, which was disfigured by
a carved clock, so magnificent and tall that it
appeared quite out of place. Yorke was, in a
manner, disappointed by the sight of the clock.
As he walked forward, Kendall espied him, and
came to meet him.

The portières of the living-room were drawn
apart, showing Penelope and Van Arsdale in
coldly critical attitudes before Loys, who was
reclining in a broad, white wicker chair, wrapped
in Penelope's evening cloak, which was of some
rich white material, heavy with fur.

" It should make a good picture," announced
Penelope, slowly. " You will wear that quaint
white gown of yours, and the cloak must be
slipping from your shoulders. Oh, here is Mr.
Yorke ! Come, give us the value of your opinion.
Sit still a moment, Loys. I do not know why

it is that Mrs. Kendall takes such an unsatisfactory picture. I can succeed with every one but her. If this one does not please me, I warn you, it will be my last attempt to transfix you."

"If success does crown your efforts, it will all be due to the cloak," observed Loys, rising. "It is capable of transforming an ugly woman into a pretty one."

Her mutable face had colored under their prolonged inspection, but she advanced to meet Yorke without a trace of discomposure. She was sincerely glad to see him, and made him feel her pleasure in a well-chosen word or two.

It was a room which wore no formidable air of order. It was lined with bookcases, and above them hung a few fine etchings, together with a picture or two by a young local artist of whom Loys expected great things. Two priceless Coula rugs (Penelope's wedding offering) served as portières, and lent a matchless bit of color. The three or four palms growing in the room were cunningly placed next the bronzes and dainty tea-equipage, for Loys was too much of an artist to be unmindful of the details of her background. Some China lilies were abloom in pretty bowls, for it was the month of February, when every other bay-window in San Francisco was aglow with these flowers ; but all the air was violet, for bunches of the California variety, with its luxurious length of stem, had been scattered about. The room was lit by the shaded radiance of lamps and the soft glow of the fire.

Kendall had taken possession of the divan, and lazily leaned one elbow upon the luxurious mass of cushions.

As Yorke was about to seat himself, Loys moved forward an inviting arm-chair, saying, " You will be more at ease here, and we wish you to be comfortable, that you may feel the desire to come often."

She seated herself near him, at the same time passing Penelope a cut-glass dish which contained chocolates.

" You might as well be introduced to all our bad habits at once, I suppose," she went on, doubtfully, offering Yorke the sweets. " I am afraid we begin to nibble candies as soon as we have finished dining."

Afterward Yorke learned to know that the little dish was always supplied with sweets, but that when it was offered to a guest making a first call, it was the signal that Loys had admitted him to her friendship. She thought people became better acquainted while eating.

8

"Am I not to have any candies?" asked
Kendall.

"Do exercise some restraint," admonished
Penelope. "You know what we told you a
while ago."

"They insist that I am growing too stout,"
explained Kendall, "and want me to ride a
bicycle. What do you think, Yorke?"

"That the pruning-knife might be applied
judiciously," hazarded Yorke. "You know,
you can carry a good thing too far."

"My mouth, for example," cited Penelope.

"If you would only walk down town in the
mornings," Loys recommended. "But the
hills are appalling, I admit, and with a cable
line on almost every street, it is next to impossible to hold to one's good resolutions to
walk."

"It must be very comfortable to eat as much
as one desires without an uneasy vision of the
extra pounds of flesh," sighed Kendall, from
his lounging-place. "Is n't it, Van Arsdale?"

Loys moved uneasily. She detested per-
sonalities. Kendall's bland question, however,
excited only a laugh, for Van Arsdale's tenuity
was a jest of old standing.

"It is," Van Arsdale returned. "By the

way, to-day I heard the most unkind remark passed upon me since the time some one said I was to be arrested for having no visible means of support. A friend of mine wondered if I did not answer Thackeray's description of George IV., — 'a waistcoat, an under waistcoat, another under waistcoat, and then nothing.'"

"Who could have told you?" cried Penelope, naïvely.

"It was you then?" murmured Van Arsdale, amid the laughter.

Penelope flushed angrily at her stupidity and tried to fasten upon the one to whom she had made the luckless remark.

Yorke came to her rescue by referring to the concert they had all attended the previous night, and then they fell to speaking of San Francisco's backwardness. Yorke was the city's only champion.

"To me San Francisco has forged ahead artistically," he affirmed. "The creditable art loan exhibitions you have had, and of which I have heard, show there are a number of fine pictures in our midst. It is true, we have only the nucleus of a museum, but the rest will come with time. And I know that twenty years ago New York was almost destitute in that regard also.   The dramatic taste of the public here is discreet, although unreliable.   It is in music that you have made progress, though I know you will not admit it, because you were unable to support an excellent though low-priced orchestra.   A few years ago the symphony concerts, which were so well attended, would have proved a signal failure.   Why, Van Arsdale, you must remember when Emma Abbott was the ideal of the city, and the music critic of our best paper exhausted his vocabulary of flattering epithets upon her, and was forced, upon hearing Patti, to confess his former ignorance."

Loys lured him on to speak of the Lamoureux concerts, and he played a *morceau* or two to emphasize or illustrate some point.

"The feeling of professional jealousy rife here will tend to keep you back," he went on. "The musicians should learn from the organizations of musical centres that every violin cannot be first, that — "

He paused, listening to the sound of a piano, which could be heard as distinctly as though it were in the next room. The others were equally silent ; only Kendall moved impatiently.

"It is the piano next door," he volunteered,

as the last note died away. "On that side our
house is wedged close to the adjoining one, for
we wished every available inch we could gain
for the lawn. Loys has got us into the habit of
keeping silence when our neighbor plays that
song."

"It is heart-breaking," exclaimed Penelope,
petulantly, striving to throw off the spell of the
music. "Do you know what it is, Bishop?"

"It is quite unfamiliar to me," he returned.
He played the closing bars, then frowned:
"You are right, Pen; it is heart-reaching.
But how is it that you do not know the name of
the composer?"

Loys awoke from a dream at finding herself
addressed.

"We are not anxious to know our neighbors,
and, you see, it would be quite impossible for
me to ring their bell, and, if the musician
opened the door, to sing a few bars of the
song, inquire its name, and come away."

He played the haunting bars once again;
they clung to his memory with tenacious
persistence.

It was growing late, and Penelope drew on
her gloves in anticipation of Mrs. Luttrell's
arrival.

"Are you going to Mrs. Boyson's cotillon to-morrow night, Penelope?" asked Van Arsdale.

"No; we expect you to come to amuse us," she returned.

"Who is Mrs. Boyson?" queried Yorke. "It is a new name to me."

"An extremely intelligent woman, who is painfully clambering up the ladder of society," explained Penelope, revolving before the glass in a last tour of inspection. "I once overheard her inquire for some *retroussé* silver, — she prides herself upon her articles of *vertu*."

"She may lack grace of manner, but she is a truly good woman," interposed Van Arsdale.

"We do not doubt it, though we would rather be left in ignorance of the fact," Penelope acceded, "for when a woman of her stamp is good, she is oppressively so. I hate uncompromising goodness."

"If she only entertains, the young people will look upon her as God-sent," laughed Yorke. "Or are the hostesses more hospitable than was their former wont?"

"Probably more entertaining would be done if the men accepted the invitations without so much the grand manner of conferring an honor," pursued Penelope. " For days here they leave one awaiting a reply to a dinner invitation, and yet they pride themselves upon their acquaintance with *les convenances*. Don't laugh to-night when you see me being led through the figures by boys in their nonage ; the only men in the rooms will be the officers from the Presidio. Your age will not militate against you to-night, Bishop."

" Henry James's problem, ' To whom shall we marry our daughters?' has reached here then," observed Yorke. " Well, as we grow more and more luxurious every day, it is not astonishing that marriage is relegated to the lower circles. Ah, here is the carriage."

Yorke enfolded Penelope in her cloak, and Loys gave the last touch to her hair.

"Try to hide the fact that you deem yourself superior to your partners, Pen," were Van Arsdale's last words.

She unfurled her huge white fan, and swept him an exaggerated courtesy.

" It would not be becoming for me to assume an air of imperturbable wisdom. It would accord ill with my length of years."

" Good-night, dear," said Loys to Penelope ; " do not work too hard at enjoying yourself."

"Poor old lady," purred Penelope to Mrs. Luttrell as she entered the carriage; "it is cruel to keep you up so late."

"This is all done for your benefit, Bishop," affirmed Mrs. Luttrell. "For weeks at a time she has kept me from bed until the stars have faded from the sky, and never before was there a murmur of compunction. What do you think of Mrs. Kendall?"

"How did she ever come to marry Gregory?" he demanded. "Did she not know?"

All the light and warmth died out of Penelope's face.

"It seems impossible to believe she did not know what was so well-known; but I do not think she did. Even after her marriage, Riker said she must have been aware of it, but he is no longer so confident. In all innocence we have heard her discuss subjects which make us, with our knowledge, turn faint and sick at heart. Every time I touch Gregory Kendall's hand, I feel myself the greatest hypocrite in the world. I have to pretend that I like him to have the right to be near Loys, but I loathe — What good do my words do?"

Yorke's face had grown set and stern. They were silent for a time, then Yorke, to divert them, said, "Why, why has she that clock in that small hall?"

"Oh, that clock!" laughed Penelope. "If some one would only steal it some night, how relieved Loys would be. You see, old Mr. Kendall heard her admire ours, and he straightway ordered the handsomest one he could find. Loys has to be very careful in what she says before him, for he gets her everything for which she expresses a desire. He worships her as much as does Gregory, only there is something pitiful in his love. The clock is a nightmare to Loys; she thinks it gives people a wrong impression of her."

"Why doesn't she place it elsewhere?" inquired Mrs. Luttrell.

"For fear of wounding the old gentleman," answered Penelope. "As a usual thing, I hate to acknowledge that there are others better or wiser than I, but I freely confess that Loys is."

Chapter X.

꜒

PON his return to San Francisco, Yorke was engaged in gathering together the loose ends of his many interests, for he discovered that his affairs required his own supervision if he wished to enjoy the right to spend money freely, — the one purpose for which he valued it. He was given to saying that he suffered from a constitutional "inclination to do nothing," yet his consuming energy made light tasks before which others would have faltered.

At her suggestion, he had taken up his residence with his step-mother. She was a coldly intelligent woman, who had lavished upon her husband the one love of her life, and yet contrived to render him exquisitely wretched.

All unselfishness impossible to her was alike impossible to every one else, although she conferred upon Bishop Yorke, because of his father, a greater latitude than she permitted others. She had never been guilty of a single warm impulse, and consequently thought all uncon-

ventionality vulgar. Yorke made no attempt
to revolutionize her theories, but was forced to
assume a quizzical air of infinite amusement
at the absolute monarchy the two women had
formed.

Upon Yorke's advent, Riker Van Arsdale
found his way once in a while to the Yorke's.
He confided to Penelope Browning that he
found Laura shallow. Penelope arched her
brows in wonderment, and warned him that
shallows are often dangerous.

Yorke entered his mother's sitting-room that
afternoon, saying, " Laura, Pen and Van Arsdale
are outside, and we would like you to go to
the Park with us."

" Did Penelope propose my going? " she
asked.

" Yes. We called for Mrs. Kendall, and
when we found she was not at home, Penelope
said we must come for you," he answered, with
stupid truthfulness. On the instant he realized
his blunder.

" Thank Pen for her thoughtfulness," said
Laura ; " but, after all, now that the horses are
ordered, it will be as well to use them, and I
know mamma will not go without me."

" Of course you know best," granted Yorke.

If Laura had expected him to coax her, she had made a mistake. He never tried to coerce any one ; he thought his friends possibly knew their own minds better than he could know them.

"Penelope is completely infatuated with Mrs. Kendall," observed Mrs. Yorke. "She always had a strange liking for original people, and I suppose Mrs. Kendall simply made her literary work the staircase to her higher ambitions."

Yorke regarded her in eloquent dismay. For once he was not amused by her original mode of thought. Words trembled upon his lips which he restrained with difficulty. Of what avail would it be to hurl his diatribe at her? It would fall ineffectually upon her blunted senses. She was quite unable to comprehend the enormity of her offences.

"I suppose Penelope's peculiarity can be accounted for on the ground that she is John Browning's daughter," mused Mrs. Yorke. "He never was happy unless patronizing some one."

"John Browning never was guilty of patronizing any one," corrected Yorke, with ominous quiet. "And Pen is quite conscious of the favor she enjoys in Mrs. Kendall's friendship."

"My dear Bishop, you forget," reminded

Mrs. Yorke, with a smile of superior pity, "that Mrs. Kendall is the daughter, I believe, of some poor farmer in Contra Costa County — "

Yorke basely fled, murmuring something about having kept Penelope waiting too long.

He laughed impatiently as he gathered up the reins.

"You are laughing at some stupidity of your own," Penelope divined. "You did not tell Laura we had gone for Mrs. Kendall?"

"That is exactly what I did," he acknowledged, with conspicuous cheerfulness. "I am confident I do not know a man who would refuse an invitation simply because it had first been tendered to another."

"Surely you do not expect a woman to be gifted with the same degree of logic as a man," she protested. "I wonder where Loys could have gone. It is not her afternoon to read to her old gentleman at the Old Peoples' Home, nor to go to the hospital — "

"To hear you, one would think Mrs. Kendall spent her life in ministering to the halt," remonstrated Yorke.

"Was I making her out a tiresome saint?" she laughed. "Well, let me modify my statement by saying that the old man to whom Loys reads is a blind English journalist, from whom she says she learns more than from any one else ; and she has an insatiate appetite for knowledge. No, Loys is not fatiguingly good."

"You and Mrs. Kendall really make a man believe that friendship is possible between women," commented Van Arsdale. "I have laid the most plausible pitfalls for you, yet I have never succeeded in insnaring the one into speaking evil of the other. By the way, Penelope, how is your pupil getting along?"

Penelope flushed painfully, as though detected in some wrong-doing.

"I used to think you made a confidant of me," he pursued. "I am hurt that you no longer let me behind the scenes."

"There is nothing much to tell," she contrived to murmur. "She cannot afford lessons, and it would be impossible to offer to pay for them, so Loys proposed that I become her teacher; and as Loys rarely asks anything of me, I assented. You see, I really deserve no credit."

Van Arsdale let his gloved hand fall upon hers for an instant. "No," he conceded, softly ; "no, you deserve no credit at all."

Penelope thought she had never seen the

Park in better mood. It is always clothed in impeccable freshness ; but that day, to Penelope, the ever-changing greens of its dense leafage, the well-kept grass, and the velvet-coated flowers nodding gently in the just stirring breeze, seemed something she had never seen before.

The driveway was gay with carriages, although a thoroughly well-appointed equipage was the exception, not the rule.

"Is n't that Loys with the Underhill children?" cried Penelope, pointing down a side path.

"Why can't you take the horses, Van Arsdale," asked Yorke, "while I go back to find Mrs. Kendall and persuade her to come with us?"

A few yards farther on, Van Arsdale took the reins, and Yorke turned his steps toward the children's playgrounds, where Penelope thought Loys had probably gone.

When he reached the grounds, he could descry Loys marshalling her young friends to the merry-go-round. The two older children elected to sail in the boats. Loys took up her stand next to the youngest child, who was astride a horse. Her back was turned to Yorke, but he could see that she was trying to induce the little girl to cease her sobs. The child would not be quieted, but obdurately continued to point to the charger beside her own.

Loys's lips were slightly compressed as she mounted her horse, but one rebellious dimple showed she was alive to the ridiculousness of the situation.

The merry-go-round was now in motion; the boats careened gayly, the animals tossed their heads bravely to the rhythm of the weird noises evolved from the internal organs of the machine. As the circle was described, Yorke saw that Loys was upon the most spirited steed of the cavalcade. Perhaps the music inspired him with ardor, perhaps his fair burden. He seemed almost to rise on his painted hind legs as he curveted along, and Yorke, who had grown slightly confused by his unrestrained laughter, and the courtesying of the ungainly monster, imagined he could perceive the wicked gleam of his eye. Loys kept her seat, not through her superior horsemanship, but because she had wound her arms tightly round the neck of the animal.

Yorke leaned against a convenient post, in a very ecstasy of mirth. People looked at him pityingly, but he was blissfully unconscious of his own antics. Again Loys swept into view; but at sight of her face Yorke stilled his laughter. She was absolutely colorless, and her eyes were closed. The rotary movement suddenly ceased, and the children clambered down from their perches; Loys dismounted with majestic composure. When Yorke saw her quivering lips he took her arm.

"How cruel you were to watch me," she cried, a tremulous little break in her voice. "You never took your eyes off me."

"But there was only one ring to attract my attention," he protested, in innocent surprise, "only one peerless equestrienne."

She laughed as she dropped his arm, saying, "The world has stopped going round — to me."

They retraced their steps to the music-stand, where they found Penelope and Van Arsdale awaiting them.

Loys did not wish to drive, as she saw that the cart would not accommodate them all, but her objections were overruled. Yorke installed the little girl upon his knee. She was a beautiful child, three or four years of age, whose charming manners endeared her to every one.

Yorke asked her her name.

"Loys talls me Baby Blue Eyes, 'tause my
eyes is blue, but my wight name is Elizabeth
Gwant Underhill.   I know what Elizabeth begins with.   It begins with a E."   She looked up
to note the effect of her astounding knowledge.

"So it does," replied Yorke.   "I wonder if
you know the letter with which my name
begins, — Yorke."

After a moment's consideration, she shook
her head.   "But I know Stephen's letter, —
it's S, — and Fweddie's letter is F.   They are
on our stockings.   Do you want to see?"

Without more ado, she brought up one
ridiculously small foot from underneath the robe,
and displayed a neat little German "E" in
red, which was sewed to the inside of her
stocking.

"Will you tell me your letter now?" she
went on.

"It is Y."

"Y, Y," she repeated to herself.   Then she
added, "That's the most cuwiosest letter, is n't
it?   It always asks so many questions."

"I wonder if your hand can do what mine
can," mused Yorke.   "Now, you see, it is
closed, but if you blow on it three times I think
it may open."

She puffed out her little cheeks, and blew and blew and blew, until she was as red as the rose Loys had tucked in her belt, and Yorke's hand opened.

" I can do that too," volunteered Freddie.

" Let's see," urged his incredulous sister, resuming her hard work, this time over Freddie's hand, and, much to her astonishment, with the same result.

" Close your hand now," prompted Yorke, " and let us see if it will not open when I blow on it for the third time." But with all his blowing, the little maid's hand remained clenched.

" P'w'aps if you blowed four times," she herself suggested. Yorke again blew in vain, and the little boys laughed at their sister's density; but she was not at all dismayed.

" I dess it's dust my will, that my marmee says 'll have to be bwoke. When she wants me to go to bed, some times my will don't want to go, but I do, 'tause my popsy don't love me when I don't mind. Me and my will has awful times."

She prattled on and on, talking of the ocean and the horses and the people, until she tired herself out.

"My eyes dust won't stay open," she confided. "I fink I'll have to button them tight.
May I go to sleep with Loys?"

"May I kiss her?" Yorke asked of Loys,
who nodded assent.

"Do you want to be tissed like Loys? It's
hard; it might hurt you," the child warned.

York preserved an undaunted front, and she
clasped her arms round his neck and pressed
her dewy lips to his.

"When I tiss Loys like that, she wishes she
had a little dirl dust like me, and me and my
marmee pways — "

Yorke silenced the child by a kiss, and laid
her in Loys's arms, where she soon fell asleep.

Penelope now entered into the conversation,
and they were all so merry that Loys's silence
was not especially marked.

"The children are to stay with me for a few
days, as their mother must have absolute quiet,"
explained Loys, as she alighted at her own door,
and Penelope and Van Arsdale drove away.
"They are going to have their dinner at once.
Will you come in?"

It was then only five, and Yorke entered
with them. The nurse took the children away
to wash them, but soon the three hungry little

people were seated at the table, and at their invitation Yorke also ate with them. They never forgot that meal, nor did Yorke, though he remembered it for another reason than theirs.

When he had performed his last trick and sung his last song, he went away. The children followed him to the door, and watched him until, at the corner of the street, he turned once more to bow, then passed out of sight.

The sky was already stained with the orange shadows.

A few moments later, Kendall reached home, and as Loys met him in the hall, he said, " I wonder what is the matter with Yorke. I passed him just now, but he did not see me. He looked like a thunder-cloud."

Then they joined the children, and Kendall romped with them until the nurse bore them away to bed, and he and Loys sat down to dinner.

Chapter XI.

꙳

KENDALL rose lazily from the depths of the arm-chair in which he had been ensconced.

"If I were not to sing, I should not have the courage to venture out," he declared, listening to the monotonous patter of the rain against the window-panes. "I don't believe I shall go, anyway. The Jinks will get along without me," he murmured, sinking back into his chair.

Loys smiled confidentially at the handkerchief into which she was embroidering his monogram.

"But will it not spoil the whole affair?" queried Helen Sargent.

"Perhaps it would," acceded Kendall, assuming a tone of seriousness, "so I presume it is my duty to go. Don't suppose you have blinded me; I see how anxious you and Loys are to be alone. By George, I have n't a cigar," he added.

Loys laid down her work, saying, "I know where I put the box."

"I'll get it myself," he remonstrated, trying to restrain her from leaving the room. Neither would return, and it ended by the two of them running upstairs for the cigars.

"You might just as well have let me go alone," panted Kendall, as they returned, and he struggled into his top-coat.

"So might you," she reminded. "Sometimes, I almost believe that you missed your vocation. From the amount of stubbornness you possess, you must, originally, have been intended for a mule."

"Pray, why could n't you give in?"

"Simply because I wish you to learn that you cannot always have your own way, sir. Then, again," she confided, "I like to make home pleasant for you before sending you off to Bohemia. I realize full well the danger I am fronting in sending you from me; but at the club there will be no one to divine your wants, as I do."

She stood leaning lightly against him, regarding him with gravely demure eyes.

"What a little fraud you are!" he protested, lifting her face to his.

Helen Sargent could not avoid overhearing their conversation, which was being carried on in the hall. Her breast stirred with dull pain; she wondered if she, too, would ever be as happy as Loys.

"Now we shall be quite cosey," Loys declared, after seeing Kendall to the door. "What has been fretting you, dear?"

"I am tired of it all," Helen broke out, her handsome face kindling with a sense of her wrongs, "so tired of the monotony of it all, that I am almost tempted to say I will marry Mr. Hawkes."

With an effort, Loys restrained a movement of apprehension.

"It is the rain," she said, "and the overwork which has brought you to this frame of mind. To-morrow you will not be in this mood."

"Perhaps not," allowed the girl, "but this mood is getting to be my normal one. I know the rain has something to do with it."

"Of course it has," agreed Loys. "You left home early this morning and walked three or four blocks to get your car, holding up your skirts in one hand and your umbrella in the other. Petticoats are an awful nuisance in the rain; you cannot keep them spotless, no matter how careful you are, and that is enough to spoil one's day."

" Then it cleared at one, and when I left school at half-past three, I met throngs of well-dressed women, and I was morbidly conscious of my rainy-weather gown. The children acted like little demons, as they usually do after being kept indoors at the recesses, and I had not a second to myself. Coming home in the car, after giving my private lesson, I met Mrs. Woods, who leaned across to ask me, in a tone which could be heard from one end of the car to the other, if I always worked so late. What is the good of going round publishing the fact that I work? I am not ashamed of it; in fact, I am rather proud of earning over a hundred dollars a month, for it proves I cannot be entirely without brains; but there is no sense in advertising my bondage."

Loys's face was alive with sympathy. Helen Sargent had a peculiar interest for her; she saw in the girl her self of two or three years ago.

" It is all very well to speak of this democratic America of ours," the girl hurried on, " but there is no such thing as democracy. I

am tired of being patronized.   I can remember
the time when we still had money, and the
difference between our treatment then and now
rankles.   I confess I am weary of the constant
struggle to make both ends meet."

"If you could only do that, you could make
your fortune in some circus," Loys reminded,
seeing the tension must be loosened.

Helen's face brightened for an instant.

"And Mr. Hawkes is the only escape I see,"
she resumed.   "If I had the time to practise
properly, I might be able to bear it all; but I
am exhausted at night, and my voice will not
obey the demands I put upon it.   So I have
decided to marry Mr. Hawkes, and patronize
instead of being patronized, and ride in my
carriage, and —"

"And be miserable ever afterward," supplied
Loys, firmly.   "Have you no idea of what marriage is that you calmly propose to link yourself
for life to such a man as Mr. Hawkes?"

"I should have the time and the money to
cultivate my gift," the girl reiterated, tenaciously.

"But what would your success mean if you
were his wife?" demanded Loys, breathlessly.
"It would be only dead sea fruit.   Your whole
soul is in your art; but you are a woman, too,

and you must not blind yourself to the fact that afterward, when success was yours, you would hunger for some one who could share it with you. Is Mr. Hawkes such a one?"

"He is not such a man as you could marry, but I do not dislike him ; and how often does a girl marry the man she loves? She usually marries the man who asks her, and ends by loving him."

"Does she?" deliberated Loys. "I am going to tell you the experience of a girl I once knew. Her case was not unlike yours, but she married the man who loved her, while you — do you hear me? — you are going to marry the man you love and who loves you."

"Where is your divining-rod?" scoffed Helen.

"The marriage is not to take place for many years yet," pursued Loys. "First, you are to study in Europe, and sing before all the crowned heads there, and be applauded to the echo. Who ever made a name for himself in San Francisco? In our humility we are afraid to trust our own opinions, or to pronounce well done what has not been declared so in Europe or New York. Now, are you going to marry Mr. Hawkes, with whom you have not one taste

in common, or are you going to make Penelope
happy by accepting her offer?"

"Suppose," breathed the girl, yielding, "Suppose, after all, that you are mistaken, — that my
voice will never be anything much, or that it
may fail me altogether?"

"I do not believe we are mistaken," maintained Loys; "and if your voice should fail
you —" She drew a deep breath and kissed
Helen's tear-dimmed face.

"What was the experience of this girl you
knew years ago?" asked Helen, dreamily.

Loys shuddered. "She —" She paused
as the maid admitted Penelope, Van Arsdale,
and Yorke.

"I wish she had known you," said Helen,
quickly. "You would have made her life so
different for her."

Loys smiled enigmatically.

For some time Helen sat listening to the
talk circling about her, yet comprehending little
but that they were speaking of music. Suddenly she bent toward Yorke, saying: —

"Will you listen to me sing, and tell me what
you think can be made of my voice? I am
asking a great deal, but I should appreciate
your opinion. I have read many of your arti-

cles on music, and I realize what your opinion
would be worth.   Miss Browning has offered to
send me to Paris, but if there are not great
possibilities in my voice, I should prefer not to
go.   I can bear the truth now better than
later."

"Would it not be well to wait until another
time?" Yorke suggested.   "You are over-
excited.   Let me come to you to-morrow."

"I shall do my best now."

Penelope rose to accompany her, vividly conscious of Van Arsdale's eyes upon her.   She
wondered who it was who said the greatest
pleasure is to do good by stealth and have it
found out by accident.

"Do not attempt anything too ambitious to-
night," cautioned Yorke.   "Will you try this?"

Loys was trembling with excitement before
the girl began to sing Schumann's "Ich Grolle
Nicht," then a great calm stole over her.
Helen was right, — she was doing her best.

When the song came to an end, and Yorke
called for different fragments from numerous
operas, to gauge the compass of her voice, his
eyes mutely encouraged Helen.

"You can make what you will of your voice,"
he declared, at length.   "I know something

of the drudgery and the disappointments and
the small chance of success, yet I advise you to
go, for I believe you will triumph. You are
extraordinarily gifted. You are young and
strong, and your personality will help you," he
affirmed, as matter-of-factedly as though he
were discussing a statue.

"There is a radical fault with your breathing," he went on. "You must lay aside all
your tight swathings when practising."

He promised her letters to people whose
very name inspired her with awe.

"Let us have tea now," urged Penelope.
"My nerves require strengthening."

"We shall have to make toast, for this bread
is not quite fresh," said Loys, returning from
the kitchen.

Penelope made the tea, while Yorke and
Loys, armed with toasting-forks, held the bread
over the bed of red coals. Suddenly the bell
tingled, and Loys, stealing a hasty glance about
the room, exclaimed, "Who can it be? Will
you go to the door, Mr. Van Arsdale? Jane is
out, and I am afraid our new cook has retired."

A moment later, Dr. Haswell stood in the
room.

"What is going on?" he cried. "A picnic?

I stopped before the door a while ago to listen
to Miss Helen, and promised myself I should
come in later before going to the club. There
is going to be toast, and there is nothing I like
as much as hot toast," he went on, usurping
Loys's place. " How is it you are having tea so
early ? "

" I suppose because we do not arrange everything by the clock here as do the Bigelows,"
Loys answered. " Mrs. Bigelow once told me
that Mr. Bigelow put his right foot into bed
every night at half-past ten, and I inquired,
thirsting for information, ' And at what time
does he put in his left foot ? ' Since then, Mrs.
Bigelow bows very frigidly."

It was a very merry little feast, and at its end
Yorke insisted upon gathering the dishes together and carrying them to the kitchen. Then
glasses were brought, and Helen's success was
drunk in champagne.

" You will live successfully through all the
hard work, Miss Helen," prophesied Dr. Haswell. " You are the fittest ; you will survive.
What do you mean," he continued, glowering
at Loys, " by writing such a morbid story as
that of yours in ' The Cycle ' ? There are to be
no more of that kind. You are to make my

patients laugh ; do you hear? and you are to laugh yourself while writing them. It would have been a better story — though it might have been sinning against all the canons of art — if you had brought it to a happy conclusion."

" It is more a study in heredity than a story, and it could not possibly have ended happily," Loys protested. " Because of the fixed laws of nature which decree that a child must suffer for the father's sins, and because of her environment, she could not escape the end. The story is not a bright one, but to me it concludes well. With her death the chain was broken, the misery was not to be perpetuated farther."

" It must be time for you to go to the club," interrupted Penelope, hurriedly.

" Don't you wish you were going to the Low Jinks, too? " ventured Dr. Haswell.

" Indeed, we don't," retorted Penelope. " We understand they are to be very low."

> "' A paradox I know it seems, but 't is a truth sublime,
>   That a man may get down very low, yet have a high
>   old time.' "

quoted Yorke.

" Loys, did I say only this evening that life was not worth living? " whispered Helen Sargent, on leaving. "Oh, Loys, no wonder you are so happy when you make so many others happy! I am intoxicated; I do not know whether it is the champagne or happiness."

Loys was tired when she finally reached her own chamber. She loosened her hair and slipped into a tea-gown, then, taking a candle, passed through Kendall's dressing-room to the apartment which opened off it.

It was a dainty room, all in white bird's-eye maple, which had originally been fitted up as a nursery. Loys stood at the head of the little crib, looking down at the unpressed pillow.

"Why can I not be as happy as Helen thinks me?" she reflected. "If the little one had lived, it would all have been so different. Perhaps now she would have been stirring, and I should have held her in my arms and soothed her to sleep again. What pain a little child's fingers could keep out of one's heart! I almost wish Dr. Haswell had not told me, — though possibly it is better I should know the inevitable."

She leaned over the cradle as if about to kiss the little face which should have rested there, then caught up the candle swiftly, and retreated to Kendall's dressing-room.

10

"I must give the cradle to some one," she breathed, with difficulty, pressing her hand to her heart. "It is wrong to encourage myself in this pain."

"Why cannot every one be like Penelope and Mr. Yorke? His letters will make matters so much easier for Nell, and his manner of offering them was so delicate," her thoughts went on, as she mechanically slipped Kendall's links into his cuffs. "He has such great, strong ways, any woman might— I am tired," she broke off, aloud. "I shall go to bed." But she made no move.

"I am glad Riker Van Arsdale heard of Pen's generosity," she continued, smiling reminiscently. "If I only dared to tell him — but I don't. I believe, too, it will all end happily without my interference. Was it Balzac who said, 'Love is a game at which one always cheats'?"

She took up the magazine in which appeared the story Dr. Haswell had so ruthlessly attacked, and tried to read it impartially.

"Despite what he said, I agree with the critics: it is the best short story I have yet written," she argued. "It is strange, but when Dr. Haswell was speaking, not one of them came to my assistance; they all preserved a chilling, disapproving silence. Mr. Yorke has discussed my other work at such length, it seems odd he should not have mentioned this. No, it is not a pleasing story; but I do think the workmanship good."

When she finally reached bed, she gave herself up to the delightful pastime of planning Helen's future. It seemed but a short time later that she heard a carriage stop before the house, and then Kendall enter. At the threshold he stumbled, and Loys heard him swear softly at his own awkwardness. He turned on the light, and, glancing over at the bed, perceived she was awake.

"Did I waken you?" he asked, contritely.

Ordinarily, Kendall's voice was of remarkable sweetness. That night it sounded muffled and indistinct. He sat down on the edge of the bed, and rested his head on his palm. Loys drew away, her face distorted by a spasm of pain.

"Yorke's paper was the success of the first part of the evening," he announced, "and Charlie Richmond's imitations were splendid. Yorke and Van left early, and they 'sisted upon seeing me to the carriage. I'm 'shamed of myself, 'shamed you should see me. I think I drank too much," he confided, gravely.

Then he commenced to laugh foolishly as the remembrance of some dubious *bon mot* of one of the wits of the club flashed into his confused thoughts.

" That was a good one of Whiting's," he rambled on. " I 'll tell it to you. It 's rather —"

" I do not wish to hear it," she insisted, sharply. " I think you had better go to bed."

" P'rapsh I had," he agreed, looking at her with owl-like solemnity. " I say, Loys, you 're looking handsome — No need to be so angry, m' dear."

Loys lay motionless and sleepless. She had never before seen Kendall under the influence of wine, and it filled her with disgust. She wondered what Van Arsdale and Yorke thought when they put him in the coupé. Being a woman, she could not be expected to know how differently a man regards an occurrence of the kind, and that Gregory's head was much steadier than those of many of his fellow club members at the same moment.

She thought she had been asleep for only five or ten minutes when she was awakened by her own cry. She was gasping for breath.

The room was hot to suffocation and filled with smoke.

She shook Kendall by the arm, calling him loudly. He was awake on the instant, and conscious.

" If only the stairs are not on fire," he cried, springing up. He hurriedly got into some of his clothes, and went round to assist Loys.

Afterward she remembered that he was calm and self-possessed. The halls were full of smoke, but no flames were visible, and they made their way to the street. The lower floor of the adjoining house was in flames, but its inmates had escaped. It was clear that the fire had not yet communicated itself to the Kendall's house.

As the cool night air struck Loys, her excitement lessened. She clutched Kendall's arm, crying, " We forgot the servants." She looked at him eagerly, as a child looks to one much older and wiser than himself, for help.

" The firemen will soon be here. There will be time enough then."

" They must be saved now, now," she persisted.

She gazed at him in stupid incredulity as his grasp upon her arm tightened, then broke away, and ran up the steps. The cries of the people in the street reached her, but she closed the house door behind her and fled through the lower hall. She paused before the cook's room, which adjoined the kitchen. The woman had already been roused by the noise, and opened the door to Loys's rapping.

"I am going to call Jane," Loys said, making her way up the rear staircase, through the blinding smoke.

The woman called to her, but what, Loys did not hear. The flames had now broken into the lower hall, and she was intent upon reaching Jane.

She beat the door of the room with her slender hands, and called and called, but there was no response. She turned the door-knob noisily to and fro, until it seemed impossible that the maid could still be asleep. Suddenly the door opened, — Loys had opened it herself, — and she stood within the now brilliantly lit room only to see that the maid's bed had not been occupied. Then she remembered that she had given Jane permission to remain with her mother that night.

She sank down on a chair, pressing her hand to her madly beating heart. She knew she ought not to rest, but was powerless to move. It seemed very quiet and restful in the little room, and the street was all alive with noise. She was dimly conscious of the fact that her arm was paining her, and she looked down at it. Above the elbow the sleeve had been burned away. She recollected that as she had made her way through the hall, a little flame had shot through the wall and leaped at her, but she had had the presence of mind to beat the fire out with the shawl she yet held in her hand.

She continued to sit motionless, listlessly wondering where Gregory was and what he was doing, and why she had looked to him to arouse the servants. Why should she not have thought at once of doing the work herself? Was his life less precious or sweet than hers?

What would the firemen think of those dishes Bishop Yorke had piled up on the table? What a gay little supper they were having now that Helen had scored such a success! She frowned at Gregory's loud laughter as he raised his glass to drink to the girl. But suddenly they all grew very still as Helen rose to sing.

It was very strange, but, somehow, she was singing the song of the girl next door, and some one was beating time to it with an axe — and —

❦

DR. Haswell and Bishop Yorke went home together from the festivities at the Bohemian Club. Their route took them in the direction of the Kendall's house, and their progress was impeded by the fire apparatus.

The two men stepped from the carriage, and saw that the Kendall's home was in flames. There were murmurs in the crowd about them that a woman was in one of the burning houses, and as they pressed anxiously forward, they saw Loys carried out.

In an instant Dr. Haswell assumed command, and, placing Loys in the carriage, directed the driver to Penelope Browning's.

The household had already been aroused by the fire. A few moments later Loys was in bed, but it was some time before Dr. Haswell succeeded in restoring her to consciousness.

At last she lay back upon the pillows, looking about her, then suddenly she started up, crying, deliriously, " He did try to save them, but I pushed him back. Do you hear, he did try. No one is to think Gregory a coward."

In the short drive to Penelope's, Kendall had given an unvarnished recital of what had taken place. He had not tried to shield himself, freely confessing that in his excitement he had been unable to think of any one but themselves ; but now, as Loys's words sounded in his ears, he cowered away from her.

"Loys, I did not save them," he began.

The physician looked up at him pityingly, then said, "Hush! She is to have her own way about it. Send Yorke to me. I shall need assistance in bandaging Mrs. Kendall's arm, and I know Yorke can render it more ably than you in your present state."

Kendall found Yorke in an adjoining room with Penelope and Mrs. Luttrell.

"Haswell wants you to help him bandage Loys's arm. Don't refuse, man," he exclaimed, as Yorke retreated. "She will not even know you are there, for she is delirious. Come."

Still Yorke made no movement. The two women looked at him in astonishment. It was a moment at which the conventionalities might well be laid aside.

"Go," Mrs. Luttrell directed. "You can probably aid him better than we can."

Nothing remained for Yorke but to obey.
Like a man in a dream he followed Kendall
into the room.

Kendall made a hasty step forward, crying,
" She has fainted again."

The physician looked up from his work angrily. " I want quiet, — do you understand ?
— absolute quiet. I can rely upon you, Yorke.
Hand me the articles as I require them."

In the meantime, he was again bringing Loys
back to consciousness.

The right sleeve had been cut from the
night-robe, and the upper portion of the arm
was swathed in linen ; but from the elbow down
the flesh showed, white and unmarred, against
the delicate blue of the silken coverlet.

Yorke had not understood his own reluctance
to obey Kendall's request, but in the unbroken
quiet of the sick-room he awakened to a perception of the truth. He was face to face with
the fact that he was in love with Gregory
Kendall's wife. He felt he had no right to be
there, yet he could not retreat.

At Dr. Haswell's motion, Yorke drew back
into the shadow of the draped bed, as Loys,
with a long-drawn sigh, opened her eyes.

" I am going to bandage your arm now," said

the physician, leaning over her, "and then you are going to sleep."

"Yes, but first Gregory must go from the room," she said, holding out her hand to her husband. "Go to bed now, so that you may be able to take care of me to-morrow. I do not wish you to see how ugly my arm looks, — you are to think of it as it was."

"You had better go before I put you out bodily," threatened the physician, moving from the bed for a preparation of cocaine.

Kendall bent over Loys, whispering, "Do you forgive me for my cowardice? Do you love me still?"

She tried to sit up among the pillows. "You were not cowardly; you were about to enter the house when I pushed you away," she insisted excitedly. "Don't you think I can remember what occurred as well as you?" She slipped her left arm about his neck, and pressed his face to hers. "Good-night, dear," she added.

Kendall turned away, not ashamed of the tears in his eyes.

"And now," said Dr. Haswell, moving to the bed, "Now, we shall take care of the arm."

"Close the doors, please. I do not wish

them to hear me, and I am afraid I shall cry: it is paining me so much now."

"Yes, I know; but it will pain less in a few moments. Be sure to help me by your bravery. It will soon be over."

His skilful fingers were already on the bandage. Loys closed her eyes and clenched her teeth, to repress a moan. Without clearly realizing what he was doing, Yorke leaned over and looked at the scarred flesh. He drew back, white to the lips, trembling in every nerve. He handed the physician the different articles as they were required, but he had no knowledge of his movements.

"Hurry," Loys breathed once. It seemed to Yorke that the physician was exulting in the time he was taking.

At last the task was completed, and Loys lay back, white and exhausted, trying to smile.

"Don't laugh at me," she implored. "I know I cannot bear physical pain. But once I moaned so loud I heard it myself; it seemed as if it must be some one's else moan, it was so distinct."

"I did not hear you," affirmed Dr. Haswell. "There, close your eyes, and sleep will soon come to you. I am going to stay with you a while."

" You are not to remain all night, as you did last September, even after you had promised to go home," she remonstrated, wearily, closing her eyes.

Dr. Haswell smiled up at Yorke, but received no answering smile. Without one backward glance, Yorke passed from the room.

" Was there much pain?" demanded Kendall, who stood without the door.

Yorke nodded assent. " Her arm — It is awful to witness a woman's pain and feel yourself helpless to lessen it. If she had moaned, I could have stood it, but she was so brave — " His voice broke.

Neither Penelope nor Mrs. Luttrell knew of any good he could do by remaining in the house, as Dr. Haswell had signified his intention to stay with Loys all night.

Yorke shuddered as the night air struck him.

He walked on and on, heedless of the direction of his steps. Twice he found himself before Penelope's door. The faint glimmer of light in the upper room attracted him irresistibly. He seemed impotent to resist its puissant spell.

Bishop Yorke had never pretended to be a whit better than his fellows. He had run the

gamut of pleasure, but he had never dwelt on
any particular note.   At that moment of intro-
spection, he was glad to find he need be
ashamed to look no man or woman in the face,
— he must take heed that he could make the
same boast in the future.

He had once declared that to love was a
waste of time, and he had lived too full a life to
waste time.   When he had planned his future,
there had always been a woman in it, — his
ideal woman ; he was not yet so old as to have
parted with his ideals.   Although he had scoffed
at love, he had believed in it so firmly as to
think it should be the foundation of marriage.
Now he suddenly realized that he must have
been egotistical, for he had never considered
the possibility of his falling in love with a
woman who would not love him.   As usual, it
was the unexpected that had happened.

He had drifted into love unconsciously, but
he must no longer continue to drift.   He
would pluck out this love from his heart.   It
would soon die when it had nothing to feed
upon ; and he would give it nothing, he resolved.

Chapter XIII.

❦

PON investigation, Kendall found that it would take some time to repair the house, although the upper portion had not been seriously damaged. It was discovered that the building itself had suffered far more than the contents.

It happened that a small furnished house next to Penelope Browning's was vacant at that time, and Kendall rented it until such time as the carpenters could complete his own.

Penelope and Mrs. Luttrell were inclined to quarrel with him on this account, for they would have liked to keep Loys with them ; but she agreed with Gregory in saying it was better for them to be in a home of their own, adding, —

"You will be with me whenever you like, for we shall be quartered almost on your lawn."

"Now, Penelope Browning, prepare to give a full account of yourself," commanded Loys one morning as Penelope made her entrance.

"Why did you not come over last evening? To what wilder festivity didst thou go?"

"I was punished for not coming. Francis Grant called, and you know how dishearteningly good he is."

"How can he help it, poor thing?" demanded Loys. "You know it takes two to be bad."

"He is pathetically homely, is he not?" acceded Penelope, with unkind readiness. "It is a sin for any woman to be as ugly as his mother."

"Isn't she very peculiar?"

"It is worse than that. Why, why, she even likes to speak well of her friends, and so does he; so you can imagine what an hilarious evening we had. That is always the way; when I try to punish some one else, I succeed in punishing only myself."

"What had we done that we were to be punished?" urged Loys. "We had one of our old-time evenings, what Gregory calls one of my country 'variety performances,' where each artist is expected to contribute a song or a dance."

"I did not come for fear Riker Van Arsdale would think I came simply to see him. He has not been near me for two weeks, and he must have remembered that he half promised to drive with us last Saturday; but I saw him with Laura and Mrs. Yorke. Was Bishop here?"

"No; I have not seen him since the day he came to inquire about my arm, though he has sent me several boxes of flowers."

Penelope absent-mindedly covered and uncovered a *cloisonné* box which lay on the table beside her.

"Loys," she commenced, "do you know any of Riker's likes or dislikes from anything he has ever said?"

Loys pondered a moment before answering.

"No, I cannot say that I do know his tastes at all except in art. He eats whatever is put before him; but unless his attention were called to it, I do not believe he would know whether he were eating fish or fowl. He comes here, but probably that is because we ask him to come, and it is as easy — perhaps easier — to say 'Yes' than 'No.' I never heard him vilify any one, but neither does he go out of his way to commend any one. Now that you mention it, I do not think I ever heard him indulge in a personality, except about you or Mr. Yorke, or that I ever heard him speak un-

less he were spoken to, though he does not seem
to be one of those alarmingly silent men. Perhaps, when he was young, his parents instilled
into his mind that children should be seen and
not heard, and he has never been able to rid
himself of his early training."

"It was not that.   Did n't I ever tell you his
story?"

"No.   What about him?" demanded Loys,
with all a healthy man's or woman's love for
personal gossip.

"I know only the skeleton of the story.   It
seems that when he was about thirty, he fell
in love with a woman, who, I suppose, would
be termed an adventuress.   Of course, he
was not aware of this, for all was outwardly
correct.   She was extremely cultured and ac-
complished, and all that, and he proposed.
But she had also foolishly fallen in love with
him, and instead of marrying him, as might
have been expected, she showed him the closed
chapter in her life, — is not that beautifully
put?   I have to give my imagination free rein,
because I do not know what really occurred,
though I think I can surmise.   In those days,
Riker was unrighteously proud of his spotless
name ; and as he had not then begun to wear a

mask, no doubt he showed her what a blow the revelation was to him. But his love was stronger than his pride, and he succeeded in overcoming her scruples. It was agreed that they were to be married at his aunt's home. You never met Mrs. Pennell, did you? No, she has not been here in the last five years. The majority of people call her a 'crank,' but it would not be a worse world if there were more like her. She reads Shelley, you know, and thinks all virtue negative, and — where was I? Oh, yes. Well, Mrs. Pennell countenanced the marriage ; but a week before the wedding day the woman quietly killed herself. Love makes us do droll things, does it not?" she ended, as she arose to arrange her veil before the mirror.

"And since then," she resumed, at length facing Loys, " Riker might have posed for that king in the old reader, — do you remember that king who has been handed down in history as never smiling again? You look as if you could not summon up a smile. Don't you know, young woman, that it is the greatest foolishness to allow the troubles of others to be anything but a dream?"

"Some one ought to save him from himself. It is not natural that any one should still feel so keenly a blow which fell ten years ago. We all humor him too much. Something ought to be done," Loys announced, with pleasing promptitude.

"Yes, but what?" queried Penelope, gathering fortitude from the look of inspiration which found birth in Loys's eyes.

"Well," commenced Loys, haltingly, "we should not speak to him unless he spoke to us, nor — "

Penelope gave an ecstatic little cry.

"You are an angel," she proclaimed. "Riker Van Arsdale shall be saved, and I shall save him." Here Penelope arose with fine dramatic effect, looking tall and slender, not unlike another Joan of Arc. "If I only knew when he intended to honor us!"

"Did I not tell you? He intends to dine with you to-night."

Penelope left Loys in peace the remainder of that day.

Mrs. Luttrell refused to countenance the project Penelope had formed, saying it would terminate in the loss of Van Arsdale's friendship; nevertheless she remained firm, or stubborn, and it so fell out that Van Arsdale and Penelope dined alone.

She made no allusion to his neglect; in fact, she said little or nothing. She was as icily cold as the soup, which Van Arsdale ate without a glance of surprise at its frigid temperature.

That evening she realized, as never before, how much he had been humored. They did not exchange five remarks during the course of the dinner, and the terrifying silence drove her, despite her resolution, into making three of them herself.

He stolidly ate the abominably prepared food with as much appetite as any meal of which she had ever seen him partake.

They sat opposite each other in the drawing-room in dreary silence. Penelope was filled with a nervous inclination to laugh at the ridiculous picture they presented. How idiotic they did look, sitting there, without a word, — exactly as if they had been married some four or five years !

"There were quite a number of people at the Kendall's last night," Van Arsdale finally volunteered.

"Yes ; Loys told me."

Another pause ensued, during which Penelope looked wistfully at the latest novel lying upon the table, which she wished to discuss with him.

But she was not yet ready to capitulate. Her courage was strengthened by the fact that Mrs. Luttrell had prophesied defeat for her, and said that she intended to listen at the door.

Van Arsdale at length took up one of the magazines she had been reading before dinner, which had been left open, face downward.

"Can you not find something more worthy of your time?" he began. "The emanations from this woman's pen have not even the merit of originality. She has stolen a thought here, an expression there, and coupled them together by foreign words, and this *mélange* is served up to catch the attention of the illiterate. Surely you saw the poverty of thought, of true art, beneath its ostentatious dress?"

She said nothing for a time, looking pensively into the fire; then, as if with a mighty effort, she faltered, "You know, I wrote it."

He could frame no excuse for his scorching criticism; he felt it to be warranted, but, inadvertently, he had hurt her cruelly. He could think of nothing to say, and silence reigned for a little.

"I did not think it so poor. Do you think it would appear so to every one?" she appealed, raising her dewy eyes to his.

"No, no," he protested. "You know I am apt to be hypercritical, and I could not have been in a responsive mood when I glanced through it."

She held out her hand, with a heart-broken little smile, which made him fancy Blue-Beard a chivalrous gentleman compared with himself.

"You need not look so regretful. You have not dealt me a death-blow." But she caught her quivering lip in her teeth and turned away from him.

"Do not take my words so much to heart," he pleaded. "What do I know about an article of that description? I am sure it must be well conceived and written, else it would not have made its appearance in those columns. Penelope, tell me I have not pained you."

She had never seen him so concerned, yet she wished more fervently than ever that Mrs. Luttrell had not kept to her threat. She turned to him, her face working not with grief, but with laughter.

"O Riker Van Arsdale, are you not a most credulous being!"

He could not understand what had changed her grief to sudden merriment. Why did she call him credulous and laugh until she had to

place her hand over her wildly palpitating heart?
She could not speak, but lay back in her chair,
her breath coming in little bursts.

"Could you not see I was jesting? I never
wrote anything."

He was immoderately relieved that it was
not her work he had so severely scored, and
then he became indignant at the deception
practised upon him. He had held the offend-
ing article until then ; but it now slipped to the
floor and lay there unnoticed. All the warmth
died out of her face, — this time Penelope had
carried her love for jesting too far.

"Do not be dignified and proud," she implored. "I could not resist the temptation to
tease you."

"It was a needlessly cruel action," he began ;
then his mouth relaxed into a smile which
threatened to develop into a hearty laugh.

She slipped off her chair, kneeling on the
floor, and, clasping her hands before her, said :
"Will you forgive me if I promise never to do
so no more?"

His face burned as she knelt to him. The
next moment she was back in her chair, re-
gretting her attitude.

"I should be versed in your wiles, but I do

not believe I ever shall be, nor do I believe in your 'never no more.' By the way, are you aware you made a mistake?" he asked, with rather a sorry attempt at pleasantry.

"You know it was through a grammatical error that Dickens came to believe in spiritualism," she said.

" Yes?"

"Yes; he attended a séance, and requested the attendance of Lindley Murray. 'Are you the spirit of Lindley Murray?' he asked, and the spirit said, 'I are.'"

The fallen book caught his fastidious eyes, and, without having to stoop for it, he replaced it upon the table.

"O grandmamma," she cried, with swift daring, opening wide her dancing eyes, "what long arms you have!"

Van Arsdale opened his lips, then closed them firmly. He declined to say, "So much the better to hug you with, my dear." He arose hurriedly; at that moment his face was almost gray.

"I promised to meet Yorke at the club. How good you are, Pen, to let such a stupid old fellow as I am take up so much of your time. You must not let me do it in future."

He looked at her eagerly, but she did not perceive it.   She was taken up with the import of his words.

" Pen, my — "   He made a step forward, and came face to face with a mirror.   At the sight of his own reflection, he drew back.   The marked contrast between them chilled him.

" Good-night," he murmured, passing out.

When Mrs. Luttrell came in a few moments later, Penelope was still standing where Van Arsdale had left her, a somnolent smile on her lips.

" Well, did you succeed?" asked Mrs. Luttrell.

" I do not know.   It is too soon to tell."

" Did he speak at all? "

" He did nearly all the talking.   O old lady, dear old lady," she went on, putting her arms round Mrs. Luttrell's neck, " you would have laughed, — laughed as I am laughing now, if you had only seen us sitting here."

But the strange thing was that Penelope was not laughing, but crying softly, and neither she nor Mrs. Luttrell knew it.

Chapter XIV.

LOYS saw Yorke only once between the night of the supper and that Monday afternoon when she met him at Helen Sargent's.

Kendall remarked upon his absence, and when he met him, upbraided him for his neglect; but Yorke urged his business cares, saying that he went nowhere, being engaged at night upon a course of papers for one of the scientific monthlies. Although Kendall did not doubt that he was much occupied, he knew he was not altogether a recluse, and he asked Loys if she had shown him any coldness.

"I am quite sure that I did not. He must have grown tired of us. It seems almost incredible, — almost impossible, I grant you; but that is what must have occurred."

Sometimes she saw him as he and Penelope returned from their rides, and sometimes as he drove past with the Underhill children; but in her notes of thanks for the flowers he sent

her, she did not ask him to call, feeling that
he knew he would be welcome, and not wishing
to seem to press him. But she gave some
thought to his sudden default. They had
grown very intimate in their short acquaintance,
for they were exceedingly congenial. Being a
widely read and travelled man, he had helped
her much ; but she now felt that the enjoyment
had been all on one side.

When she reached Helen Sargent's that afternoon, Mrs. Sargent ushered her into the parlor,
saying nothing of Yorke's presence. Helen had
resigned her position as teacher, and was busily
preparing for her early departure. Upon seeing
Yorke, Loys would have withdrawn.

" Don't go," cried Helen, interrupting her
breathing exercises. " We were just finishing."

" I shall detain you only a moment. I saw
this in the White House this morning, and I
think it is what you want for your travelling-
gown," Loys continued, showing Helen a sample
of dress goods. " It is like the Mongolian
conscience, having neither right nor wrong
side."

" It is exactly what I had in mind. If you
are going into town, will you order it sent to
Mrs. Austen's for me ? "

"Yes. Pardon my interruption. Good afternoon, Mr. Yorke."

She failed to extend her hand, and the omission hurt him.

"May I go with you as far as our roads lie together?" he asked.

"I shall be glad to have you. I am going to take the California Street cars," she pursued, on leaving the house. "Gregory promised to take me into Chinatown if he could contrive it, and if not, to send one of the clerks with me."

"Would I do as a substitute?" asked Yorke.

At sight of her, all his brave resolutions had weakened. He had been so unbendingly severe to himself that he believed he deserved some indulgence.

"Are you sure you wish to come?"

"I was never so sure of anything," he assured her.

"I wish to get a few ornaments for Helen's rooms in Paris. If some of the articles belong to her, it will give the apartment a home-like air, and I know there is more than one hour of homesickness in store for her."

They passed some of the finest residences in San Francisco, many of which were now closed, their owners having gone away to spend their money in other places.

"I suppose you have done this part of the city thoroughly," Yorke remarked, as they entered Chinatown. "I know Penelope is fond of engineering her friends through here."

"I once went with a party of hers, but they had to take me home. The odors suffocated me. I have been in the restaurants and the shops, but I really do not care to explore further."

A band of chattering Mongolians passed them on the narrow sidewalk, and turned to stare at Loys. She slipped her hand within Yorke's arm, pressing against him.

"I really believe you are afraid," he exclaimed.

"I know it is ridiculous, but I cannot overcome the feeling. I suppose you heard Mrs. Lidderdale speak of the Chinese when she was here. I think she spent the greater portion of her time prowling about Chinatown, and she used to expand over their beautiful courteousness and their low salamings (it was during the week of their New Year that she was here) until I began to wonder if I had seen the same race of people as she."

Loys's purchases were very modest ones, but they were not necessarily any the less pretty.

"I go about distributing these boxes in the

same magnificent manner that the Queen does
her India shawls," she laughed, as she chose
a glove-box and handkerchief-box of carved
sandal-wood. "Oh, here is the mate to my
little blue vase ! Evidently no one has had the
good taste to choose its fellow. Did you notice
that it is the real Sèvres blue? How much
is it?" she asked, turning to the fat, oily
proprietor.

"Tlee dollar hap."

Loys replaced the vase on the counter.
"No, indeed," she said, decidedly. "I paid
only two dollars and twenty-five cents for the
other one."

"You pay only two dollar qlawter for him?"
leered the man, incredulously. "I gib you
this one for tlee dollar."

"We will take it for two dollars twenty-five,
and not one cent more," put in Yorke.

His tone awed the Chinaman into putting
the vase beside Loys's other purchases. He
did it grudgingly, however.

Loys added to the little pile of ornaments a
dainty piece of *cloisonné* and a carved ivory
paper-knife, Yorke conducting the haggling for
her. No self-respecting Chinaman ever dreams
of mentioning at once the price he really expects to receive.

"May I add a little gift?" Yorke appealed. "Something which can go in your package, and only be discovered when Miss Sargent is there?"

"Yes, I think you may; but it must be something very small."

He obeyed her command to the letter. It was a very small piece of Satsuma he selected, but Loys could not avoid seeing the price he paid for it. She made no demur, however, knowing the amount was no more to him than the small sum she had expended was to her.

They retraced their steps through the crowded streets, and Loys was glad to reach air which was not vitiated by the dying fragrance of decaying fish and vegetables.

"I am going to have this afternoon to myself," affirmed Yorke to himself, as they neared the library. "It is a cowardly indulgence, but I am harming only myself. I am no more to her than any other of Kendall's friends."

Loys ran lightly up the first flight of stairs leading to the library, then paused at the landing.

"I do not know what is the matter with me," she protested, laboredly. "I shall have to go up the next flight more slowly."

"It is too warm for you here," urged Yorke, as they entered the library proper.

She was glad to follow him into the reference room. They were quite alone, and sat looking out of the window, exchanging malicious remarks upon the passers-by, each with a proper enjoyment of the other's wit.

"There goes Bradbury up to the club," exclaimed Yorke, as he espied a friend. "Does he not look the typical man who lives in the suburbs, who cultivates a bit of green and a large family? He goes home at night, a newspaper package under each arm, to read his favorite political organ, while his wife placidly sits beside him, darning, and his numerous progeny perform their school tasks."

"That is not impromptu. You recite it much too glibly. I am sure it must have been embodied in some sketch of yours," Loys mocked.

"But instead of following my description, Bradbury is vulgarly rich, and unmarried," Yorke smiled.

Loys looked about the room meditatively. "There was a time when I knew those shelves much more intimately than I now do. I used to pore over those dust-stained volumes until

12

my head ached, so as to be armed for the girls' questions. Some of them used to make it a point to hunt up the most terrifying questions, simply for the pleasure of confusing me. But it did not do to betray ignorance too often, nor to say that I was not an encyclopedia. And the quotations from Darwin and Spencer and the rest of them that I knew, — no girl ever thought her essay complete without a few lines from one of them, although she would have been virtuously shocked had she read their complete rejection of her most hallowed beliefs."

"What an appalling piece of work it must have been for you to write those essays," Yorke observed, innocently.

"Did I say I wrote them? If you had ever heard a school-girl's essay you would not accuse me so fearlessly," she concluded, as she arose, and they searched among the books. "I have been having too many solids lately; I must have a novel this time."

"Let me select something for you."

"Will you? But let it be something a man will also enjoy. Gregory likes to have me read to him."

There was a pause before Yorke spoke. "What kind of a novel is a man's novel?"

"I cannot describe the kind, although I am familiar with several. Take, for instance, 'The Sinner's Comedy.' I never recommended that book to a man who did not enjoy it."

"You are right," agreed Yorke. "It is a man's novel."

Upon leaving the library, he said, "Will you go with me to get some marshmallows for the Underhill children?"

She could not well refuse, and he ordered also two boxes of marrons.

As he stood with her at her own door, he handed her one of them, saying: "Here is something for the heart-shaped dish."

She stood above him on the step, and, so standing, her eyes were on a level with his.

"That little dish is no more, but the same rules govern its successor: only those who help empty it are allowed to fill it," she affirmed. There was a half-smile in her eyes, but there was also a touch of wounded pride, and at sight of it Yorke's pulses leaped.

"I shall expect you to save me some for Friday evening," he replied, alluding to the dinner-party she was to give on that night in honor of Helen Sargent, and to which he had been invited.

She hesitatingly extended her hand for the box.

"If I told you how much we missed you, I think I might persuade you to give us one of our old-time evenings."

As her words repeated themselves to her, she reflected that the speech could have been made only by a married woman. She was surprised at her own insistence; she could not recall ever before having asked a man to call after he had once flagged in his attentions.

"Have you missed me?" he asked. Unconsciously he lowered his voice.

With an effort she averted her eyes. At that moment, Kendall jumped from a passing car, and joined them.

"I see you must have been acting as my wife's escort, Yorke," he said. "Did she buy all the pottery in Chinatown? Come in, old fellow, to dine with us."

"Thank you. I am due this evening at Whiting's. By the way, Mrs. Kendall, will you chaperon a little dinner I wish to give Miss Sargent, at the club?"

"Of course she will," interposed Kendall. "She is only too anxious to dine away from home. You know we sometimes go off on a

tour of the restaurants. You have a real fond-
ness for a 'bat,' have n't you?" he demanded
playfully, appealing to Loys.

"What a word !" she reproved. "You must
not unmask me before Mr. Yorke. Had I
known you intended to sacrifice my good name
to your boast, I should have chosen a more
discreet companion."

Her face had suddenly assumed a look of
utter weariness, although her eyes burned with
unnatural brilliancy, and her lips were a thread
of scarlet.

"Well, Yorke, when are we to have you drop
in upon us in your old-time fashion?" Kendall
urged. "Mrs. Kendall insists that it is a wound
to her pride, but that you must have grown
weary of us. Here, Loys, add your entreaties
to mine."

Yorke listened for her words with almost
painful impatience.

"Why," she said, with an irrelevant, excited
laugh, "why do you wish me to try my meagre
suasive powers if yours have failed?"

Her laugh jarred on her ears. How many
times that afternoon she had laughed, — enough
for a whole lifetime. How thoughtlessly gay
she had been ! She wondered if Yorke intended
to keep them before the door all night.

"Do you know," Kendall commenced, when they were alone, "you can be freezingly cold at times. Why did you not ask him to call, informally?"

"Did I not?" she queried. "He is coming Friday evening." She sat down in the hall, loosening her scalskin with nervous haste, as if it had grown too heavy for her.

"Have you heard that the Geralds' troubles have finally culminated in a divorce suit?" gossiped Kendall. "I am sorry for Gerald. What a fool that woman was not to be satisfied with a good man's love!"

"She was more than a fool. You cannot blame the frog who leaped from a throne of gold into the puddle, but a woman! —"

"What has occasioned this sudden change of front? I thought you always said that our vaunted virtue lies in not being tempted, and that you urged a beautiful leniency —"

"Not towards a married woman," she interrupted. "A married woman cannot continue to drift on blindly. There must come the awakening, and then she must prove herself brave and strong enough to trample the love under foot."

"Your views satisfy me. One can see you

have never loved any man but your husband. Your words sound very fine in theory. My dear child, we will suppose that I had no right to love you — do you imagine that because I had not the moral right, I could the more easily conquer my love? "

His words did not seem to reach her.

" Are you going to sit there all night? " he pursued.

" Do you know whose lines these are? —

" ' As one that on a lonesome road
Doth walk in fear and dread,
   And, having once turned round, walks on
And turns no more his head,
   Because he knows a frightful fiend
Doth close behind him tread.' "

" What made you imagine I would know? I never read a line of poetry unless you insist upon it. Ask Yorke on Friday evening, if you are curious to know."

Chapter XV

LOYS stood in the hall, waiting until Kendall should draw on his gloves, for she was going into town with him. As she waited, she recognized the postman's ring, and opened the door. There was only one letter for her. It was from her mother.

"I am so glad," she cried. "Mother is coming to the city this afternoon, and is going to spend a week with us."

Kendall studied with interest the name of his hatter on the lining of his hat.

"Why don't you wire her to wait until to-morrow?" he proposed, in a strained voice. "You must see that it would be rather inconvenient to have her here to-night."

Her features stiffened as she measured him with eyes which caused him to feel that he had lost several inches in height.

"Why inconvenient?" she demanded, haughtily.

"You said the dining-room here would accommodate only fourteen, and that you intended to have only those who would be most useful to Helen in the years to come," he explained, haltingly. " Besides, your mother will not be at her ease among the people who are coming."

" I think she will," she maintained. " I should not dream of subjecting my father to such an evening. The hours would seem interminable to him, the gowns of the women indecent, and their talk vapid. But mother will enjoy it all, and look back upon the evening as a treat. The dining-room will be somewhat crowded, but it cannot be avoided. Do not wait for me. I am going to send a note to Mr. Van Arsdale, explaining our need of him. He will come to our assistance."

Kendall muttered something between his teeth and slammed the house door after him.

" How dared he ! " Loys breathed in passionate contempt.

But there was no time that morning to give vent to her feelings. She despatched the note to Van Arsdale, then went to her florist.

When she reached home, she found Van Arsdale's reply awaiting her. He wrote that he was more than pleased that she could not do without him, for within the last two days he had regretted having said she might omit him.   He was possessed of a devouring desire to be present at the dinner.

"He does know how to confer a favor," she murmured.

At one o'clock the flowers arrived, and Penelope Browning, who had a more than amateurish talent for arranging them, came over to assist Loys set the table.

When the last flower was arranged, the last menu-card placed, and they stepped back to mark the effect, Penelope and Loys confessed themselves satisfied with the result of their efforts.

At four o'clock Loys went to meet her mother.   Penelope, who had remained during Loys's absence, disembarrassed Mrs. Yerrington of her wraps.

"Are you going to show your mother the table now?" she inquired.

"Yes.   You know, mother dear, I wrote you about Helen Sargent's going to Paris, and to-night we are giving her a little dinner."

"I wish I'd waited until the morning," murmured Mrs. Yerrington.

"You will not to-morrow," prophesied Penelope.   "You are going to enjoy a delightful evening."

Loys opened the dining-room door, and Mrs. Yerrington stood looking about her with bewildered eyes.

" Why, it 's fairy-land ! " she exclaimed, after a pause. " O Loys, I wish I had n't come to-day ! "

" I wish I had time to scold you, but I must run away, for I have a letter to write before dressing," Penelope remarked.

Loys accompanied Penelope to the door, to thank her for what she had done. When she returned to the room, her mother said : " No one knows I am here, and I 'll have a bite in my own room and listen to the music from there. I could n't be comfortable here, dear. I would n't know what to do with all these forks and glasses and things."

" In a moment you will. Now, listen." Loys explained the use of each article, and, when she had finished, Mrs. Yerrington repeated her words. She perceived that Loys would not permit her to remain upstairs, and she was intent upon doing her best.

" Do not trouble about anything," advised Loys. " You are going in to dinner with Mr. Yorke, and Mr. Van Arsdale will sit on the other side of you, and Penelope next to him, so you will be surrounded by those you know."

From the night of the fire Loys had been forced to have her hair dressed, for her arm was in a measure disabled. The woman came twice that day, and Loys stood over her as she arranged Mrs. Yerrington's still luxuriant hair.

Mrs. Yerrington started back in naïve astonishment when Loys at length allowed her to look in the glass. The lustreless black silk she wore had been made only a few weeks previous, under Loys's supervision, and Mrs. Yerrington had worn it only once; but on that occasion she had dressed her hair in an uncompromisingly hard knot, and a bunch of violets had not been fastened at her breast by Loys's cunning hands.

"What have you done to me?"

"I merely touched you with my wand. You did not know how pretty you were, did you?" queried Loys, mischievously, shaking out a handkerchief of cobweb fineness for her.

From the moment that Mrs. Yerrington noticed the change in her appearance, she grew more assured.

Kendall reached home as Loys was putting the last touch to her toilet. She heard him on the steps, and awaited his coming in trepidation, for she did not know how he would bear himself.

He entered the room, affecting a boyish gayety at sight of Mrs. Yerrington, with whom he was a great favorite. When he turned to greet Loys, there was a look of pleading in his eyes to which she could not remain cold. Whatever else he was, he was her husband; she could not reject his overtures for peace.

As he bent to kiss her, he whispered: "Do you forgive me? You do not know how wretched I have been on account of what happened."

She made no attempt to escape from his arms, and his face brightened. The instant he found he was forgiven, he forgave himself.

"I have brought you something to wear around your neck," he proceeded, reddening as he took from his pocket a jeweler's box.

Her features threatened to stiffen again as he showed her a string of pearls. She recoiled from the thought that he had attempted to bribe her into forgiveness. She made an attempt to receive the gift graciously, but her failure was covered by her mother's exclamations of admiration.

"I know you always said you did not wish a necklace; but this is such a simple affair that it will not hide your throat," observed Kendall, as he clasped the pearls about her neck, with a kiss.

As he went to his dressing-room, Mrs. Yerrington said: "I like to see you together. What a happy wife you are!"

"Am I not?" Loys echoed, moving the pearls as if they were too tight.

They went to the drawing-room, where Kendall soon joined them. Loys had taken a last look into the kitchen and at the table, and awaited the guests with a clear conscience; she had done her best for their welfare.

There was no dilatory one that night. They were all well-known to one another, and even before taking their places at the table there was no lack of merry talk.

From her seat Loys could see Kendall intently watching her mother, consequently she became painfully alive to her every movement. Fortunately, Mr. Whiting, who sat at Loys's right, spoke with the skill of the professional talker, and his pungent wit concealed the fact that she was doing her best to be stupid. It was a wit which was appreciated none the less because it stopped at nothing. If Mr. Whiting's auditors were sometimes haunted by the reflection that it was unkind to laugh at his unsparing remarks on their friends, they speedily redoubled their laughter, spurred on by the thought that they, in their turn, would serve him as food for his reputation of splendid daring.

After a little, Loys perceived that Yorke was careful, at the beginning of each course, to give Mrs. Yerrington her queue, in an unostentatious manner. They were chatting naturally, — Yorke rather more talkative than was his wont, but drawing more than monosyllabic replies from his companion. Penelope and Van Arsdale also joined in their conversation at times. They seemed to be having a very merry time, as they all did.

With a lighter heart Loys turned to Mr. Whiting, rewarding his efforts with smiles which bore no traces of the pain she was bearing; for she could not shut out from her sight Kendall's implacable eyes upon her mother, and Yorke's thoughtfulness.

The dinner was quoted afterward as having been one of the most brilliant of the season; but no particular credit could be attributed to Loys because of this. She had, as usual, gathered about her a group of people quite capable of providing their own entertainment. Unless there were some good reason for it, she refrained from inviting people who expected to be amused. Naturally, she preferred the man who expects to amuse.

Penelope Browning had assured her that she had made the mistake of inviting people who could talk but not listen; but that night Loys found no fault with them on that account.

She toyed with her food, but could hardly force herself to swallow a mouthful. No one else appeared to think the room warm, yet she found it stifling, and the pearls about her neck seemed to be suffocating her.

As it was nearing the time for the women to leave the dining-room, Mr. Whiting said to her: "I wish you would inaugurate the sensible plan of remaining with us while we smoke a cigar. You know it is only incense burned to you."

She wondered how many times the remark had served.

"Come," he continued, "if you are wise you will drop the foolish custom to-night."

The lights and flowers were dancing before her eyes; she was only too glad to escape from the room.

"I make no pretensions to being wise, — I could not live up to them," she averred, with a smile which would have reconciled any man to her unmitigated stupidity. She arose as she spoke and marshalled her troops from the field.

The coolness of the drawing-room revived her; but when the men rejoined them, the air soon became heated.

Loys was standing near the door as Helen arose to sing. The girl was looking triumphantly beautiful; but from her eager way of observing Yorke, Loys could not help feeling relieved that she was so soon to depart.

The lights suddenly began to waver and grow dim to Loys; and as the first note broke on the air, it seemed to come from a great distance. She made a few uncertain steps into the hall, endeavoring to reach a divan she remembered they had placed under the stairs; but the more she tried, the further it receded from her. Then she felt herself carried to the lounge and some one chafing her hands. She knew it was Yorke, but could not open her eyes.

"Loys," he whispered, in unguarded tones,

13

leaning over her in fright, "Loys, do you hear
me?"

She felt she could now speak if she made
the effort, but she made none.   After all, what
were two minutes in a whole life-time?   No
one should rob her of them.   She would banish
the thought of Gregory from her thoughts for
those poor seconds; she would —

Even as she was determining what she would
do, she opened her eyes and sat up.

"It was so warm," she faltered.

"Shall I call your mother or Ken —"

"No one is to know," she broke in.   "Probably they have not missed us."

Yorke made no movement to help her rise.
The muscles of his face were tense and rigid.

"You have done too much to-day," he said.
"You must not tax your — "

"I did nothing," she protested.   "It was
only the heat."

Van Arsdale was the only one who had remarked their absence.   He regarded Loys
curiously.   He never remembered her being
so fitfully gay as she was that night.   Usually
she was content to make others shine; but
during the remainder of the evening her conversation was spangled with wit.   With reck-

less prodigality she scattered her caustic *bons mots* into every quarter until Kendall realized the extent of her nervous exhaustion; for it was only when Loys was thoroughly overwrought that she was so madly gay.

No one seemed inclined to leave, but Yorke finally contrived to break up the gathering.

Kendall waited until Mrs. Yerrington had gone upstairs before speaking to Loys. By a deft touch here and there, she was bringing order out of the chaos which reigned.

"Stop," he ordered, as she was about to wheel a divan into place. "Jane will have time enough to arrange the rooms in the morning. You have done far too much as it is."

"I realized the dinner was a success when Mr. Whiting quoted, '*Avec une pareille sauce, on mangerait son père;*' but was it a pleasant evening? I never can determine in our own house. Were you pleased?"

"More than pleased. There was not a moment's tedium. But you are not feeling well," he said, anxiously. "What is it, my wife?"

"Put out the lights; they make the air so warm."

As she listlessly watched him fan out the last glimmer from the lamps, she came to a sudden determination.

"Do not snuff out the candles yet," she commanded. "I must tell you that I tried to pose as a heroine to-night. I almost lost consciousness out in the hall, and Mr. Yorke had to carry me to the divan."

Kendall reached her side quickly, and, sitting down, drew her to his knee.

"It was my dam— ugly temper of this morning that caused it, and I let you do too much. Tell me where the pain is. Were you unconscious long?" he asked, placing his hand above her heart.

"Not more than a minute. I felt that I was falling through bottomless space; I suppose my heart must have lost a beat. Oh, foolish one, you have grown quite pale. Then you do not wish me to die just yet?"

"Die?" he echoed, with trembling lips. "I forbid you to say that word. Have you no idea how it pains me to hear it in connection with you? To live without you, my beloved — " He hid his face upon her bosom, endeavoring to regain command of himself.

"Have I ever given you cause to regret

having married me?" she demanded, in wistful persistence.

As he took her in his arms to carry her up the staircase, he answered by a laugh, which contented her.

"And I never shall," she added, vehemently.

Chapter XVI.

❧

THEY had accompanied Helen Sargent across the bay, and seen her safely installed in the flower-laden drawing-room; so it was late that evening when Penelope and Van Arsdale, Loys and Kendall reached home. The gloom of the parting was still upon them, and they were inclined to be somewhat silent until Van Arsdale asked them their plans for the summer.

"Except for an occasional run down to Monterey over Saturday and Sunday, or a very impressive invitation to spend a few days in some friend's cottage," answered Kendall, looking laughingly at Penelope, "I think we shall stay quietly at home."

"In the good old times I believe people went to the country to wear out their old clothes," remarked Penelope. "I wish those days would return. How can men believe that women dress for them, seeing the gowns we need for the sea-shore, where, as every one knows, men are as plentiful as flies about honey. I suppose we shall have to seek consolation in the thought that, as the little boy said in his composition, the good Lord liked Eve so much better than he did Adam, there have been more of her sex ever since. What are you going to do, Riker?"

"The Yorkes have asked me to spend a few weeks at their place in San Rafael."

"Yorke is variable," observed Kendall. "He has not been near us since he paid his call of digestion."

"He has been down at his ranch the past week," reminded Penelope. "I must go home in a few moments, for he is coming to-night. The air is deliciously soft. Will you go to the Cliff if I order the horses?"

"I am too tired to-night," said Loys.

At that moment the maid handed Kendall a telegram. Murmuring a word of pardon, he tore open the envelop. He read the message at a glance, then sat staring blindly down at the words. In an instant his face had become haggard.

Loys quickly left her seat and walked round to him. He remained passive as she read the dispatch : —

" Come immediately. There is no hope. Your mother has regained her reason and wishes to see you."

It was signed " Robert Kendall " — the name of Kendall's father.

" Your mother?" Loys echoed. " Why, Gregory," she went on, placing her hand upon his shoulder, " some one is trying to play a sorry jest — "

The expression of mingled misery and pleading in his eyes killed the words on her lips. She looked at Van Arsdale, mechanically tracing a pattern on the table, at Penelope Browning, who had risen, pale to the lips. There came to her a shadowy recognition of the truth. Then she closed her eyes for a second; the overwhelming light blinded her. She shrank from the unbounded pity shining in Penelope's face. No one had ever dared to pity her before. She would have no one pity her now.

" For a moment I forgot," she murmured.

Kendall passed the telegram to Van Arsdale, explaining, " My father must have gone to Napa this morning, — perhaps Dr. Newell wired for him. He did not know she was ill."

Van Arsdale looked at the clock, whose

brazen voice was plainly audible in the quiet room.

"We must leave the house within ten minutes if you wish to make the next train," he said.

He knew there would be time in half an hour, but he was anxious to escape from Loys's presence.

"I will get ready," Loys began, turning from the room.

"You cannot go," Kendall broke in. "There will not be time, and it is better I should go alone. She does not know you."

"I shall get your dressing-bag," she said.

Penelope could not keep pace with her on the stairs. Loys gathered together such articles as he would need, Penelope standing by helplessly.

"You will wire me the first thing in the morning, Gregory," she said, calmly, as she met him in the hall; "and if you find you can use me, let me know."

He did not trust himself to look at her as he touched her cheek. He tried to speak, but the words failed him, and he abruptly followed Van Arsdale.

Loys continued to stand at the open door long after they had passed out of sight.

" Come in, dear," directed Penelope.

" You left your wraps in the sitting-room, did you not ?   Let me get them for you."

" But I am going to stay with you."

" No, you are not ; you are going home now," Loys declared, impatiently.   She hurried into the room for Penelope's belongings.

" Let me stay with you. Don't send me away to-night," Penelope entreated.

" I know how much you would like to be with me, but I wish to be quite by myself."

Loys opened the door, and Penelope could do nothing else but pass out.

" I will not annoy you ; I will not even ask to sleep with you, if you will only let me stay in the house."

" How good you are ! — but you have always been good to me, Pen.   There, — go home."

Loys closed the door.   Penelope listened vainly for some sound from within, but after some moments of waiting, stole noiselessly down the steps and home.

Loys had sunk down upon a hall chair. Her thoughts were still benumbed, — she only knew she was glad to be alone. She wondered if it were only last night at the play that Penelope and she had laughed as the leading lady explained, in a speech of five minutes' duration, her desire to be alone.

Suddenly there flashed upon her the remembrance of that afternoon at Mrs. Wills, the medium's. Yes, some one had withheld something it was of vital importance she should have known. She aimlessly pleated and unpleated her handkerchief. It occurred to her that her calm was unnatural : if she had read of a woman acting, as she was acting now, she would have so characterized it. But of what avail would tears or useless rebellion be now?

She lived over again the night of her engagement. How tired she had been! She saw Kendall as he sat plucking viciously at the tassel of the chair, and combating her views on her sister's marriage. That night, too, he had had in his pocket the letter from Penelope Browning, containing the offer to her of the European trip.

Loys shudderingly reflected that Mrs. Wills had been right : she had gone with the wrong one.

And Gregory's hardly concealed joy at all of his intimate friends being out of town, and his father's coldness in London, were now explained.

Those who might have saved her had been away, or had thought she knew, and dared not speak. No one had given her one warning whisper.

His father had known what Gregory thought of her, — why had he not told her? The answer came to her readily : all along he had believed, with her, that she would never marry him.

Loys had not dared to question Penelope ; but she knew that the insanity was hereditary, else it would not have been so completely hidden from her, and they would not all have preserved such an ominous silence when she had brought forward her views on heredity.

If her child had lived — But it was foolish to try to exaggerate her troubles. Mercifully, the child was dead. As the child was dead, she could forgive Gregory. She was the only one to suffer, and nothing much mattered as only she was to suffer.

She groped her way to the stairs and slowly toiled up them. Her clothes oppressed her, and with trembling fingers she unfastened her dress, and slipped into a white woollen tea-gown. She shuddered as her fingers came in contact with her body, — they were icy cold, and her face was burning.

" I shall take my bath now, instead of later.
It will warm me," she decided, walking to the
bath-room.   She turned on the water, and
stood watching it as it welled up higher and
higher.   There recurred to her the stories she
had heard of death by drowning.   They all
agreed that it was a pleasant death.   The tub
was more than three-fourths full, but she made
no movement to turn off the water.   To think
that by merely holding one's head under it for
a few —

With an effort she tore herself away from its
fascination, and ran into her room.   The maid
was there, arranging the bed for the night.

"Please turn off the water, Jane.   After all,
I shall not bathe now."

She covered her eyes with her hands, drawing a long, quivering breath.   She cowered
away from the thought which had been with
her a moment before.

The house-bell tingled.

"It is Penelope," she thought.   "Was she
afraid of this that she was so insistent?"

It was not Penelope's voice she recognized:
it was Yorke's.

Loys restrained an unseasonable desire to
laugh.   What had Penelope feared, that, after

her rude treatment, she had not ventured to come herself, but had sent Yorke? In another moment her anger was dissipated. She had no right to deprive Penelope of her rest when she could quiet her simply by receiving Yorke.

She descended the stairs. One glance at his face convinced her that he knew.

"You are in trouble," he exclaimed, standing at the foot of the stairs, and she a step or two above him. The subdued light of the lamp above her clearly marked the dark shadows about her unquiet eyes, the tense muscles of her mouth.

"Yes: Gregory received a telegram from his father that his mother is dying, but conscious," she explained. "It would have been more merciful, I think, had she gone without recovering her reason. She has not seen Gregory now for, for — "

"I think it must be quite ten years," he supplied, not appearing to notice her hesitancy. "The sight of him only disturbed her; and though she did not recognize her husband, she was glad to see him."

"Yes, so I have heard. Of course we did not speak often upon the subject, so I must appear very ignorant; but was she violent or —"

"Only melancholy," put in Yorke, quickly. "At first she remembered Mr. Kendall and Gregory at times, but during the past fifteen years she has known no one," he went on, thinking it wiser that she should know the truth instead of torturing herself by her imaginings.

"I wish, oh, I wish she did not know them now!" she whispered. "To think that she should recognize them only now, at the end, and know all the closed years behind her. It is pitifully sad to think of, is it not?" she demanded, dry-eyed.

"You are not to think of it," he commanded, roughly.

"She will hardly recognize Gregory," she continued, monotonously, unheeding his order. "In fifteen years he must have changed a great deal. Upstairs I have a faded picture of her, taken shortly after Gregory's birth. She is holding him in her arms, and her face is lit by such a look of mother-love. She must have been very beautiful.

"I must not keep you standing any longer. Are you going back to Penelope?" she continued, without any clear knowledge of her words. "You will tell her that I am going to bed at once."

"That is wise," he remarked, not disputing that he had just left Penelope. "Mrs. Kendall, will you not permit Penelope to remain with you? It will be much better for both of you, and it will comfort her to think you wish her with you now."

"But I do not. You must go now."

He could think of no excuse to urge for his continued presence, although when he was without the door a number of reasons came to him.

When Loys regained her room, the sinister quiet of the house wore upon her.

She sank wearily down upon the couch. She would go to bed as soon as she had rested a moment.

She hoped Gregory would reach there in time. It would be too cruel if his mother should be deprived of one last look at him.

She held the photograph which she had mentioned, and thoughtfully studied it. She wondered if Mr. Kendall had known of the taint in the blood at the time of his marriage. Suddenly, from out the storehouse of her memory, there came the recollection of a fragment of conversation between Gregory and his father that she had overheard in London.

Mr. Kendall had said, "I shall never forgive you this;" and Gregory had demanded, "And have I nothing to forgive you? You knew it before you married, and still it did not prevent — "

At the time, Gregory had, in some manner, explained the words to her; now she no longer needed his explanation. Everything was illuminated by one awful fact.

As she continued to look down upon the pictured face, the horror of the whole thing broke more fully upon her.

"I cannot bear it," she cried, pushing the picture from her. "If she had only gone without realizing what had happened; but to think of her now, trying to comprehend all that has passed, and only understanding one thing. It is maddening to think of. Poor woman!

"I must be calm," she pursued, as in her excited march up and down the room she caught sight of her figure in the glass. "I must be calm for their sake. When it is all over, they will look to me for comfort, and I must be able to give it to them. They will expect me to — "

14

She laid her head on the cushion. "If I could only put the sight from me," she murmured. "He said it was a private asylum, but the shriekings and the — I shall go mad myself if I persist in this," she broke off.

Every nook and corner seemed to be alive with uncanny sounds. She was afraid to raise her eyes. Why had she not permitted Penelope to remain with her, or Jane? Where was Bishop Yorke? She had begged him to stay with her, but he had pushed her aside. Only Gregory was good to her, and now he was mad. No, not mad, but she must laugh and talk a great deal to keep him from becoming melancholy. Oh, yes, she would laugh. What mad laughter it was. But did not King Solomon write, "I said of laughter, it is mad"? What a whirling dance her thoughts were leading her !

When she recovered consciousness, she was lying on the floor. After a little, she got to her feet, and walked to the glass. There was an irregular blue mark on her temple, — evidently she had struck against a chair in her fall.

"I cannot breathe in this house," she asserted, sullenly. "I could sleep if I were at home.

I always slept well during vacation. They will be glad to see me, and mother will help me undress, and kiss me after I am in bed. I know I shall sleep there."

She made ready for the street, and, turning off the lights, walked out of the room. The house was then in utter darkness save for a faint-light in the lower hall.

At the corner of the street she paused, but after some moments, awaking to the fact that it was so late the cars had ceased to run, she turned her steps toward town.

Behind her she heard distinctly the regular footfall of a man, which broke, with exaggerated sound, upon the stone flagging; but now that she was on the street, she was no longer afraid.

San Francisco is essentially a city of hills, and the Kendalls lived in one of its highest portions. The heights Loys climbed that night would have been, at any other time, almost impossible to her, for she was not a sturdy walker; but now she moved on without pause.

Yorke kept a few feet behind her, ready to spring to her side should there be need of him. Now and then a baker or a milkman rattled by in his wagon, but otherwise they met no one; and Yorke was willing that she should thoroughly tire herself, when he thought she might, of her own accord, retrace her steps.

They commenced to near the livelier portions of the town, and Yorke felt that he ought to declare his presence and take her home, yet shrank from doing so. A moment later a man stepped from a neighboring doorway, and, peering into Loys's face, observed, "You're out late, my pretty one."

The salutation effectually wakened her. She shrank back as Yorke stepped forward and took her arm. The man had passed on.

"Come," said Yorke, "let me take you home."

"Where was I going? I remember now," she pursued, putting her hand to her head with a pitiful little gesture. "I was going to mother."

"Yes, but we are going home now," he rejoined.

She made no motion to turn. Her lips set into a hard line of determination; but Yorke grasped her arm firmly, and set her face homeward. Once she endeavored to wrest herself free from him, saying, " I will not go back. Do you hear? I will not go back."

He only held her the more securely, affirming, with unswerving decision, "You are going back."

"Going back," she repeated, drearily. "Do you know to what you are taking me back?"

But even that insidious question did not sway him.

There was not a vehicle of any description in sight, nor was there any means of procuring one, and he was forced to see her walk. They were very quiet for the first seven or eight blocks, and then her steps began to flag.

"I shall have to rest," she said at length.

She sat down upon some steps, and Yorke stood beside her. The bruise on her forehead was revealed by a street lamp, and he surmised how she must have come by it. He almost wished that she would again lose consciousness that he might carry her. The deadly exhaustion of her face and the fierce splendor of her eyes unnerved him.

They resumed their walk. Once or twice her strength threatened to give out, but she succeeded in reaching home. At the corner of the street she tried to withdraw her arm from Yorke's.

"If I need only not go back," she implored.

He affected not to hear. His lips were stiff.

"We are almòst there now," he said, forming his words with an effort, while his steps unconsciously loitered.

Not even the deadly hostility he cherished toward Kendall for his deceit made him falter in taking Loys back to him; but it was not an easy task. He knew that her present mood would pass, and that in all the years to come Kendall would never hear a reproach or murmur from her; but Yorke also realized the daily torment she would undergo, the suppression of all natural feeling, and at that instant all his soul revolted at the sacrifice he was countenancing and even dictating. But a saner moment showed him there was no other road open to her. After all, Kendall was her husband, and she could do nothing to put her name in the mouth of the world. She was a woman ; her hands were tied. She would continue to live on with Kendall, giving the outside world no cause to doubt her happiness, and making her life a decorous sham, as was demanded of her. And Kendall would be quite happy, and she —

With desperate courage Yorke fitted the latch-key in the door and opened it. He paused uncertainly in the hall, unwilling to leave her alone in the dark, empty house, but feeling that she could not now call the servants. His mind was not so elastic as usual ; it worked with confused laboriousness.

"I shall light your gas for you," he said at last.

She offered no objection, and he went up the stairs, into the room, and made it ablaze with light. He was not anxious for her to have the darkness for company. He did not stay to look about him, but hurriedly rejoined her in the lower hall.

The expression of her face had changed during his absence. All the drawn hardness had left it. She was again as he had always known her. One gloved hand rested upon the newel post for support. She raised her head at his approach.

"I have given you much trouble to-night," she began, in her usual low voice, though there was now an undercurrent of utter fatigue in it, "but I shall not attempt to thank you, for I know you were glad to help me when I so much needed a friend."

"We are friends : we always shall be friends."

Her hand rested in his in perfect confidence. That he loved her she knew, but she also knew that she had nothing to fear from him. From that night on he would understand her great need of friends, and not deprive her of his friendship.

"You must retire now," he went on, in a tone of authority which admitted of no appeal. "Make the bed look as though you had occupied it, and when you are ready, call the maid, saying you have grown nervous. I shall wait here, in the shadow, until I hear her go to your room; then I shall go away. Goodnight."

She made no demur; she was completely dominated by the spell of his stronger nature.

As he was about to release her hand, there came to him the full significance of their parting. He turned her hand until it lay with the palm up, then reverently bent his head and kissed the flesh, which lay there like a crumpled rose-leaf.

She went up the staircase and disappeared. After a time he heard her pass into the hall again, and shortly return with the maid. Then he left the house.

His brain was reeling. He suffered the more keenly because he felt his own helplessness. If he could only lessen her burden, he imagined he could bear his own grief more bravely. There recurred to him her last words. Yes, she needed friends, and she wanted him for her friend.

"Friend?" he breathed, in cynical derision. He could not deceive himself as to his feeling toward her when every nerve was tingling with love. Yet it was only by being her friend that he could be of service to her. He must blot out all this mad longing, which dishonored his friendship with Kendall. He must —

He recoiled before the utter hopelessness of it all.

Before he turned his face homeward that morning, he had battled with himself and imagined he had come out victor. At least, he had not flinched from the hard truth. He saw clearly the incalculable harm his love could bring her, and he was resolved to be her friend.

A servant was washing down the marble steps when he reached home. The man stood looking after Yorke until he disappeared into the house.

"He's been having one of the devil's own nights of it," he mused, "and he's paying for it now with a racking good headache. But you've got to pay for everything in this world, — one way or the other," he concluded, with a wise shake of the head.

Chapter XVII.

ENDALL was gone only two days. On the third morning he returned home unannounced. Loys chanced to be walking through the hall when he entered the house.

"Is she — " she began, advancing to meet him.

"No," he corrected, quickly. "No; she is alive. All danger is past, but she no longer knows either of us."

She forced him to lie down on the couch, and then she brought a flask of eau de cologne, and bathed his brow.

"When you are rested, you shall tell me about it," she said. "But now you must sleep."

"I cannot sleep," he protested. "You do not know what I have undergone. I would not wish my worst enemy to go through such scenes as I have witnessed. To see her trying to fathom out all that had taken place, and then, when she was beginning to pierce the darkness, to have it envelop her again. Great God! It was awful; it was maddening. Loys, what must you think of me —"

With all her feeble strength she pushed him back upon the cushions. The wildness of his eyes filled her with paralyzing fear.

"You must go to sleep," she dictated. "I shall bring you a light breakfast, and then you must try to sleep."

He arose, and, grasping her arms, faced her.

"Do you know what you are thinking?" he demanded, vehemently. "You imagine you already see in me the seeds of my mother's disorder. But I am only exhausted from the loss of sleep and the strain put upon me. I do not know why, but I feel certain my mind will never become affected. Don't turn from me. I sinned against you, but my love was stronger than my consciousness of what was right; and even knowing all the misery I have brought you, if I had to do it all over —"

"Hush! You must prove your love for me by lying down and letting me take care of you."

"I think I could bear your reproaches better than this," he exclaimed, covering his eyes with his hand. She stood motionless and cold.   With sudden passion he drew her down beside him.   .

"Do you hate me, or do you love me ?" he questioned, holding her with cruel firmness.

There was a throb of wild rebellion, which soon passed.   Her life was to be a living lie : she must not shrink from the beginning.   She put from her forever the oppressive longing she had to speak the truth.

"After you are rested, you will see that you must not put such questions to your wife," she said.

"Of course, if the little one had lived, I know you could not forgive me, nor would I myself.   But she did not.   We are all alone, and there is no reason why we should not be happy, is there?"

And she answered, "None."

In a week Kendall had apparently forgotten all that had transpired.   He always contrived to convince himself that he was more sinned against than sinning.   At first he seemed to harbor some resentment against Van Arsdale and Penelope for having been present that night, and once or twice he murmured petulantly that he would appreciate their society more if they were not favored with so much of it.

Loys did not try to combat his feeling. She, too, longed to escape from them. She seldom detected Van Arsdale's eyes upon her, yet she thought she understood the sensations of a fly impaled upon a pin being studied under a microscope.

She had never cared for the theatre unless the play were an exceptionally good one; but they now went to every representation, good, bad, and indifferent. She so arranged matters that they rarely spent an evening alone. At last Kendall rebelled.

"It is all very well to have people dine with us twice, or even three times, a week, but I am not going to have some one here all the time. We are not conducting a restaurant. Recently we have been staying up too late. You cannot stand it. Van Arsdale told me to-day that I ought to send you away for a time. He insists that you are not looking well."

"Perhaps I was wearing an unbecoming gown when he last saw me," she suggested.

The explanation did not satisfy him.

"You have grown thinner," he resumed, "and I am not surprised that it is so. You go to bed at indecently late hours and get up at indecently early ones. You must go to Del

Monte with Penelope, — or would you prefer to go over to the cottage in Ross Valley?"

"I am not going to Ross Valley," she declared, a sharp intonation of pain running through her voice at the remembrance of the preceding summer spent at the cottage; nor am I going to Monterey without you. I can afford to lose a little flesh. I used to term myself plump, but probably my enemies called me 'fat.' Is not that an abominable word?"

In her flittings in and out of the house at all hours, Penelope surprised Loys at times, as she lay extended on the couch, neither sleeping nor working nor reading.

"You have grown shockingly lazy," she admonished. "How can you lie idle when there is all your new table linen to embroider? You do not take enough interest in yourself. Bishop Yorke asked me the other day if one had to be disabled in order to arouse your interest. It is all very well to help the poor, but you need not give up your whole life to them. Why don't you spur on your jaded Pegasus to renewed flights?"

"I sent off the manuscript of my novel only a week ago. Do you wish me to turn out a story a day?"

"I do not know. Perhaps I am in a fault-finding mood, but lately you have not seemed so bright — "

"And this after last night," opposed Loys, "when I imagined myself the light and soul of the party; when I strewed before you my choicest pearls of thought, my favorite anecdotes. Ah, this is an ungrateful world! No, Pen, I shall confess. You have merely grown too well acquainted with me. I used to have the knack of putting the witticisms of others into my own chafing-dish and serving them up before the same public in such disguised form that they were unrecognizable; but I suppose that with old age the vein has become exhausted."

"Go to Monterey with us, and mingle with the brainless mob for a time," pleaded Penelope.

But her entreaties were unavailing, and she and Mrs. Luttrell were forced to go alone. Loys breathed a sigh of relief at their departure. She felt that she could now do as she liked without any kindly inquisitive eyes upon her.

She gave herself up to long days on the couch, when she did nothing but brood over her troubles and vivisect her own emotions; but Kendall knew nothing of her mood, for at night she was always ready to amuse him. She shrank in horror from her own thoughts, — that they were only natural made them none the more excusable. To be so tired that she could not think! and she filled her days so full of duties that she overtaxed her strength.

Penelope, however, was away little more than a fortnight, every day of which she sent Loys a long letter, for which the society papers would gladly have paid any price. She was a master-hand at ridicule, and wrote with a pointed pen which spared no one. Yorke went down to see her one afternoon, and the following day she returned home.

Between them they frightened Loys into a submissive silence, and took her out for long drives, and tours of discovery about the bay and the adjoining country. She affected an interest in everything, but was unsuccessful in her efforts to impose upon them. They were aware she would have been thankful to have been left to herself.

But Kendall thought he had never seen her looking better than the night of the Townsend wedding reception. Although late in July, every one had made it a point, if possible, to return from their summer residences for the occasion.

Loys was with Whiting when they came

upon Van Arsdale with Laura Yorke upon his
arm.

"You both look surprised to see Mr. Van
Arsdale here. But we permitted him no voice
in the matter," said Laura, with a calm air of
proprietorship which irritated Loys.

"Have you missed me?" asked Van Arsdale
of Loys.

"San Rafael is not at the other side of the
globe," Loys returned. "If you had cared to
spare us chagrin, you would have contrived to
give us one evening in a whole month. At
first we spoke of your default, and threatened
to go after you, in a body. Now we no longer
speak of you. It is not because we have forgotten you, — unfortunately we are not of the
forgetting — "

"I am coming back to town. I shall return
to-mor — "

"Indeed you shall not," broke in Laura.
"We cannot think of your deserting us in that
hurried fashion."

Loys looked at her in undefined fear. She
had never felt a match for Laura Yorke, and
she was now filled with unreasoning apprehension. She looked round for Penelope, who
she felt was clever enough to outwit Laura.

"You will surely see Penelope," Loys said to Van Arsdale, as they were swept apart.

A few moments later Yorke came to claim her, and bore her away from Whiting.

"Will Townsend told me that supper is to be served in another half-hour," he said, "and he is going to have the men place a table on the east veranda, for a select party. I shall install you there, and then recruit our forces."

He found a comfortable corner for her on the veranda, and, after she had assured him that she was warm enough, he went away to gather together the chosen spirits.

Loys contentedly lay back in her chair, enjoying the balmy, flower-scented air, and the prettiness of the scene before her. She started as she suddenly heard Laura Yorke and Van Arsdale in the room behind her. Evidently they were standing at the window, but were unaware of her presence, as the high back of her chair effectually concealed her.

"It would have been a pity to break in upon Penelope's waltz," Laura was saying. "How she does enter into the spirit of gayety! She does not look nor act as if she were more than twenty, does she? I tell her that some day she will marry her English lord. His infatuation was clearly shown when he was here, and even Penelope can hardly look higher. He seems to have every desirable quality."

Van Arsdale proffered no remark. At length he said : " There she goes with Blair. Ah, well, it does not matter. I shall see her to-morrow night. I have trespassed upon your hospitality too long as it is."

" You cannot mean to leave us, when we all want you so much," Laura exclaimed, with a loss of self-possession utterly foreign to her, " and when no one has a right to demand your return to town. We shall miss you," she continued, laying her hand on his arm.

Loys hardly dared to breathe. She was conscious that she ought to do something, but she could not determine what.

Van Arsdale stood looking down at the girl's gloved hand upon his arm. Her eyes were raised to him. They were swimming in tears. He felt that something was demanded of him, but he made no movement.

" Have we bored you ? " Laura pursued, then turned away her head, to hide the tears which rolled down her cheeks.

The man, feeling himself a brute, hesitatingly made a step forward. He could no longer

thrust from him the thought which had threatened to intrude itself upon him once or twice
before.

" Laura ! " he exclaimed.

" Do not look at me," she entreated, crouch-
ing down upon the window-seat.   " Oh, I am
so ashamed !   Take me home."

" Don't," he protested.   " Don't cry.   Do
you think you love me enough to be my wife?
You must not forget my age —   Come away.
They are going out upon the veranda."

" It was too cold for you here without a
wrap," said Yorke to Loys.   " You look as
chill as a moonbeam."

She looked up at him in mute appeal.

He bent forward to shield her from the eyes
of the others, saying, " What is it?   Are you
quite well? "

" Yes, but —   Ah, you cannot help me.   Let
us be gay, gay as all the rest of the world is in
appearance to-night."

" Tell me," he entreated.   " No one is listening.   You can tell me safely."

He looked so powerful, so capable of setting
right what was so plainly wrong, that she half
swayed toward him.

" This will never do," called Whiting.   " Look

here, Yorke, we expect you and Mrs. Kendall
to help us with this array of bottles. Don't
you intend to eat or drink?"

Van Arsdale came out upon the veranda as
Penelope and Whiting were engaged in a
war of words which had stopped all other
conversation.

Loys regarded him half in anger, half in
pity. He had taken the one course seemingly
open to him: it would have required a man
with a more resourceful brain than he possessed
to have extricated himself uncommitted from
the recent encounter. Despite her generous
scorn of Laura, Loys was forced to bestow a
certain amount of unwilling admiration upon
the adroitness with which she had gained the
man she loved.

As some retort of Penelope's provoked the
laughter of those about her, a quiver of pain
stirred Van Arsdale's face.

"You forgot to laugh," he said to Loys. "I
thought you and Penelope had a pact to laugh
at each other's wit."

" I never can enter properly into the gayety
of a crowd," she returned.

"When I left Mrs. Kendall here before
supper, she was thoughtlessly gay," put in

Yorke. "When I returned five minutes later, I found her as you now see her."

Van Arsdale gazed at her with unwonted keenness. It seemed to her that his eyes demanded why she had not interceded to save him. With maddening after-wisdom, she saw how easily she might have frustrated Laura's cunning.

Then she arose, saying petulantly, "I am chilled. Let us go in."

"You have remained motionless too long," remarked Yorke. "Will you give me this dance?"

She laid her hand on his arm as Penelope came up to them.

"Will you be very much disappointed, Loys, if I deprive you of your waltz? I wish to go home. I have a headache; would you call it an aching void?"

"Wait five minutes," urged Yorke. "Now that Mrs. Kendall has promised me this waltz, I intend to — "

"I am sorry, but Loys is going to take me home now."

Loys studied her in inward questioning, wondering if some inkling of the truth had already reached her.

"Yes, let us go," she agreed, nervously.

"After you have given me one little turn," Yorke said, with sullen tenacity. The hauteur of her face recalled him to himself. "I am afraid I am in a hectoring mood to-night. But I confess myself beaten, for here comes Kendall himself."

Penelope's headache left no visible imprint upon her spirits. She was in a bright, talkative mood all the way home.

"You are not to kiss me like that again," she commanded, with a wilful laugh, as Loys kissed her good-night. "It was a kiss which seemed to say you were sorry for me."

Loys passed the night in bitter perplexity, and the daylight found her with no settled plan of action. But when Kendall had gone to his office, she ran across the lawn to Penelope's.

She was about to do a dishonorable act, but she believed herself justified in it. She would stop at nothing to save Penelope one pang. Penelope was in her luxurious bath-room, the one possession Loys really envied her.

"Is that you, Loys?" she called. "Draw your chair to the door and we can talk comfortably. Whose reputation shall we first attack? I woke up sleepy this morning, so I

shall not be so amusing as ordinarily.   By the
way, did Riker Van Arsdale speak to you last
evening?   He never so much as came near
me."

"I appeared in the rôle of eavesdropper last
night," commenced Loys, glad of the closed
door between them, "and I am going to
make you share my guilt by telling you what
I overheard."

"Wait a moment.   I shall enjoy it more
thoroughly if I see your face, and I shall soon
be ready to throw on a *peignoir*."

Her words hastened Loys.   "Did you notice
anything unusual between Laura Yorke and
Riker Van Arsdale?"

There was an almost imperceptible pause
before Penelope answered, "Well, they were
together nearly all the evening."

"And they have decided to be together for
the rest of their days," broke in Loys, helpless
to soften her words.

The connecting door opened, and Penelope
swept in.   She was still flushed from her bath,
and her hair, which had been massed at the
top of her head in a great knot, had loosened
itself from the one shell pin which held it, and
waved softly about her face.   Her beauty hurt

Loys at that moment. It seemed only to add to the bitter pathos of the whole affair.

" It was entirely unexpected on his part," Loys resumed. " He did the one thing left him to do, under the circumstances."

She briefly recounted what had happened.

Penelope listened without comment. At the end, she said : " She really deserves him for her cleverness. Possibly the plan might not have been successful with every man, but only a simpleton could doubt its success with him. And so Riker is going to be married," she pro-ceeded, musingly. " It will be hard to give him up, for virtually it will be giving him up ; his marriage cannot help but alter our relations. Do you know, it makes one feel curiously old to see all one's friends getting married. Laura always did admire him."

" I must go home," murmured Loys, rising.

" Will you do me another favor ? I wish you would go down town with me. There are sev-eral birthday gifts which might just as well be ordered to-day as later, and I suppose I ought to send a silver porridge-bowl to that Taylor baby."

Penelope usually affected the same severely simple style on the street as did Loys, but that morning she made an elaborate toilet.

She went out of her way to be amiable to
people whose existence she usually blandly
ignored.

"Penelope, my dear, which of these two
lamps shall I take?" deferred Mrs. Hamilton,
whom they met in the art rooms of the White
House.   "Presents are simply ruining me this
month.   These ain't very handsome, I admit,
but they're the cheapest they have in the
place," confessed the old lady, in whose ears
glistened, from morning until night, diamonds
so large and brilliant that they successfully
blinded many to her awful delinquencies.   She
had a fearless tongue, and a marvellous memory
for the personal history of early days, which
gained for her a degree of deferential respect
which was truly ludicrous.

"Do not spend too much money," cautioned
Penelope.   "You know there is another wedding whispered about."

"Whose?"

"Don't you know? Ah, well, it is not my
secret, but you will soon hear of it."

"I believe it 's your own, and it 's high time,
and it won't require much of a guess as to the
man," pursued the terrible old lady, peering at
Penelope in not unkind shrewdness.   "If you

had married, you would n't look so young and
free from care, but it 's about time you settled
down.   You 're my Maud's age, I know, though
no one would think it.   But that is what it is
to have three children, and a husband with an
eye for the beautiful — in other women.   But I
sha n't send you a present.   First of all, you
won't invite me, and you 've made too much
fun of my presents."

"If I were to be married, I should certainly
invite you ; I wish one of your famous lamps, —
and I never should have the courage to buy
one for myself," Penelope smiled.

A moment later the old lady's laughter re-
sounded through the apartment.

Nothing was demanded of Loys that morning.
Penelope smiled and talked for both ; but Loys
was exhausted when she reached home.

"Was there ever any one as stupid as myself?" she appealed.   "If I had only made
my presence known when Laura began to speak
of Penelope, I could have prevented what followed.   And I meant Penelope to be happy,"
she continued, in fierce impatience.   "Do I
dare?" she asked, as a sudden thought came
to her.   "Yes, I dare do anything for Penelope.
She shall be happy."

Forgetting all about luncheon, she went into town again. Her courage failed her as she stepped from the elevator in the Mills Building, and found herself before Yorke's door. As she stood hesitating, Yorke himself opened the door. There was a gleam of astonishment at sight of her, which he quickly subdued.

"I have come upon a daring errand," she finally commenced. "I am going to tell you what I tried to say last night. I have always thought that Mr. Van Arsdale cared for Penelope, but felt that she was worthy of more love than he could give her, have not you?"

"This is too hard for you," Yorke exclaimed. "Let me finish. When I left you on the veranda last night, you overheard what took place between Laura and Van Arsdale. Before she retired her better self was again in the ascendant. She has written him, saying he must not endeavor to see her, and asking him to forget what occurred. My mother and Laura start for New York to-morrow."

It was not an easy position for either of them, and Loys looked down upon the carpet to hide her tears. Yorke walked to the window.

"Do not blame her too much," he urged, coming back. "Her excuse is that she has given him her best love. As soon as he received her note, he went to the house; but Laura refused to see him, and he came to me. He accused me of having prompted the letter, but I succeeded in convincing him I had had nothing to do with it. I also told him a truth or two. I think Penelope is going to be happy."

Loys impulsively took his hand. " I am so happy, so happy," she breathed, with a tremulous little smile.

Yorke's face set in an expression of grim determination. He thought she would never rise to go.

" I have undertaken too much," he decided. " If she does not soon go, I shall forget everything but that I love her."

Still unaware of her peril, Loys left him.

She had been gone but a few moments when Kendall came in.

" I met my wife downstairs," he said. " She told me I must not inquire what her errand with you was. I am here about that Marsh lease. But, first of all, I want to know if you think Loys looking well. Haswell wishes me to send her away, but I cannot leave now, and I cannot bear the thought of being with-

out her, even for a week or two. She insists
that she is perfectly well, and she certainly has
not been in bed a day since her illness last
September. A stranger can tell better how she
looks than one who sees her every day."

"Does Mrs. Kendall wish to go away ?"
Yorke asked, shifting a paper-weight from one
side of the desk to the other.

"No, she does not," Kendall replied, triumphantly. "In fact, she absolutely refuses to
go. She used to fret a great deal more than
she now does. Formerly she could not enjoy
her day's bread without seeing to-morrow's
(already buttered) in sight, forgetting it would
do her no good to save her bread until it was
stale. She lives more in the present now."

While Yorke listened, he was thankful that
his moment of madness had been short-lived.
He was divided between pity and contempt for
Gregory Kendall, yet he was glad that the man
saw nothing of the effort through which Loys
always appeared bright and well. It was little
surprising that she endeavored to live in the
present. She was wise to close her eyes to the
future, but Yorke doubted her success in keeping them closed.

He shrank from the thought of the life of

exhausting effort which stretched before her, and he drew a sharper breath as he saw how narrowly he had escaped darkening it for her.

" If I ever cause her a moment's pain, I shall be the blackest scoundrel who ever lived," Yorke declared, when Kendall had gone. " A woman is satisfied with so little ! and as my friendship contents her, there is no harm in continuing to see her. She knows how much Kendall needs her, and separation from him has never occurred to her. She is utterly beyond me, and to speak would be to — "

His heart failed him at the utter hopelessness of it all. He buried his face in his hands, murmuring, " Loys, Loys, my love ! "

But his cry did not awaken him to the great need there was that their attempt at friendship should cease.

Chapter XVIII.

HAT same afternoon Penelope was in the garden in the rear of the house when the man brought her a card.

"I shall receive Mr. Van Arsdale here, Wilson."

"Even if you come only once a month, you must not expect to be treated with ceremony," she called, as Van Arsdale came up the path. "We are looking old and jaded, Mr. Van Arsdale," she continued, courtesying. "We cannot stand late hours, Mr. Van Arsdale. We should gracefully retire, Mr. Van Arsdale. We are growing sadly old, Mr. Van Arsdale."

But she did not look old, as she stood before him in a sheer white gown of some wash material, and the amber light of the setting sun came drifting through the foliage of the huge palm-tree behind her, and lost itself in the depth of her eyes.

"Do you know," she cried, changing color under his steady eyes, "you look as though you

had come to tell me some great news, some
secret."

"So I have."

"I am so glad! I am hungering for a sen-
sation. I wrote letters all the afternoon, and,
for once, they were dull letters. San Francisco
is such a stupidly proper place. None of
one's friends ever obligingly gives us cause
for gossip. And now for your news.

"How slow you are!" she went on indefati-
gably, seating herself on a rustic bench, while
he sat above her, watching her as she lightly
touched the queen pansies she had been gathering, in their quaint garb of royal purple. "You
really must commence, for I shall have to dress
for dinner soon, and I cannot ask you to stay
to-night."

"Can't you?" he questioned, blankly.

"No. But where is your story? You have
gotten out of practice. I remember you used
to tell nice ones in the days when I was a little
girl and you held me upon your knee." ·

"I never did hold you on my knee," he
rebelled. "To hear you, one would imagine I
was old enough to be your grandfather. It is
true, I am past forty, but you —"

"I shall be twenty-eight in two months," she
16

supplied. "But we are not going to discuss ages. I am impatiently waiting for the story."

"Once upon a time," he began, tracing a capital " P " in the gravel with his stick, " there was a man, old and ugly and morose, who dared to raise his eyes to a woman who was as far above him as the stars. He did not blind himself to the difference in their age, to her beauty, and her — "

" You must not think of that," she broke in, " I am sure it never occurs to her."

" Are you? " he asked, eagerly, taking her passive hand into his. " I never knew my great need for you, Pen, until last night, when you seemed to vanish from me. What is the matter, love? "

She had laid her head upon his knee, but the one glimpse of her face dissipated all the doubt of her love he had entertained.

" Pen, do you love me despite my years and my settled ways? Do you know what people will say? I have no right to let you do it. Are you sure you will be happy with me and the little I have to give you? "

She raised her face with sudden passion.

" I must speak now; I have been silent so long. I know you cannot give me your best

love, but I shall be content with little. I
realize what people will say; I have said it all
to myself many times in the effort to displace
you from my heart. But I cannot love any
one else but you. If you will only let me be
with you, I shall be the happiest woman in the
world."

He bent down to her as she rested against
his knee, a great flood of tenderness filling his
heart. The love he could give her seemed so
pitifully small next to that which she lavished
upon him. He drew her head to his breast.

"Even if you are asking me only in pity,"
she faltered, stealing her arm about his neck,
"I am happy."

Her words cut him to the quick. There
was a dull pain in his heart as he thought of
the woman to whose memory he had been untrue, and then he banished it.

"I am old, Pen, and there is nothing in my
life hidden from you, yet if you knew the bitter
pain I suffered last night because of you, you
would not question my love."

"Why because of me?"

"Why — Why, because you went to supper
with Blair, instead of with me," he finished,
lamely.

"How could I go with you when you did not even ask me?" she demanded, with a dazzling smile.

"Mrs. Yorke and Laura are going East to-morrow," he volunteered, pressing her closer to him. "Pen, can't you persuade Mrs. Kendall to go away for a while?" he continued. "Don't you realize how ill she is looking? By the way, do you know why she went to Yorke's office to-day?"

"Yes, I do," she returned, feeling positive she now knew to whom she owed her happiness.

"Don't you think she would be better away from here for a time?"

Their eyes met in a long glance of understanding, and her lips quivered.

"She will not leave Gregory now. I think she fears she may not be strong enough to return to him. There is nothing to dread. She will go on to the end without a falter. I am going to tell you some — something I know I should keep to myself, but — Do you know what her life is? The other day after Gregory had kissed her, I saw her shudder. She mistakes his slightest moment of thoughtfulness for melancholy, and I heard her say to Dr. Haswell, 'You must give me something to make me sleep, or I believe I shall lose my reason.' Is she right to go on living with him? Surely she has a right to happiness, too. Oh, how is it going to end?"

"Do not cry," he begged, smoothing her hair. "Yorke must go away."

"He must not go away. He is the one gleam of happiness in her life. After she has seen him, she is more as she used to be. Neither of them is irresponsible or careless of his own self-respect. We are insulting her," she broke off. "Let me go to dress for dinner now."

"You could not put on anything more becoming. I do not have to go away, as you at first said, do I, dear?"

"No. I thought you were going to tell me — At least, I did not think you intended to stay, so I made believe I did not want you."

"And you will give me the next few days, will you not, Pen?"

"I cannot," she deplored. "Mr. Bedell and his sister arrived to-day, and I asked them to go to Ross Valley, to stay until Monday."

His look of disappointment delighted her.

"On Sunday I shall invite you and Bishop, Loys and Gregory, and Mr. Browne, over for a picnic. Will not that be lovely?"

"Is that what you call 'lovely'? No, it will not be 'lovely' at all," he protested. "I am like Mrs. Kendall in my objection to crowds. I shall not have a moment alone with you, I know."

"Of course you will not, if you are not clever. But perhaps if you exercised a little wit, and I went half-way to meet you — "

He leaned down, and, as it had grown dusk, he found the courage to go more than half-way to meet her lips.

Chapter XIX

AS Penelope went over to Ross Valley on the following day, only the Kendalls and Yorke were told of the engagement. Loys found it impossible to refuse Penelope anything at the moment, and promised that she and Gregory would make one of the picnic-party on Sunday.

Penelope and her guests met them at the station with a tally-ho coach, and they at once set out. Kendall was at first inclined to deride the idea of a long drive, saying he would prefer to picnic in Penelope's own spacious grounds, or in Schaefer's Grove; but when they were fairly started, he made no further objections, for Miss Bedell divided her attentions, with impartial favor, between him and Douglas Browne, who had been invited for her special benefit.

At one o'clock they drove into the shadow of a great clump of trees, at the foot of which ran a little brook, and the luncheon was un-

packed. Loys put the graceful ferns Yorke
had cut in the middle of the table-cloth, and
piled upon them the luscious fruits, arranging
everything with the daintiness which marked
her.

They were ravenously hungry, but Penelope
insisted that Yorke was using his skill at sleight-
of-hand in disposing of his food.

"Who will reach me that freckled egg?"
Yorke asked, lazily, entirely unabashed by their
remarks. "You make me ashamed of my
appetite, Mrs. Kendall. You have been holding that sandwich for the last five minutes."

Loys started guiltily.

"Perhaps Mrs. Kendall is wiser than I, and
dreads dyspepsia," suggested Miss Bedell.

"I have always enjoyed most vulgar health;
I am never conscious of my infernal, I mean
my internal, machinery," Loys asserted.

"There is a box of candy somewhere about,"
said Penelope. "Some one please search for
it. Mrs. Kendall is never happy unless eating
sweets."

"That is all a thing of the past," commented
Kendall. "I brought a box of candy home on
Friday night, and it is still untouched."

"I am getting past the chocolate-cream

stage ; even marrons cease to tempt me. Oh,
I realize I am getting to a very certain age,"
sighed Loys, whimsically, listening to the car-
ollings of some wood-thrush in the still deeps
behind them.

When luncheon was a thing of the past, they
lay lazily about. Mrs. Luttrell, however, had
had the forethought to bring a sofa-cushion for
Loys, who was exceedingly uncomfortable if
she found her head on a level with her feet.

Yorke and Kendall and Penelope formed
themselves into a trio, and sang some sacred
music, which fell with fine effect on the curious
dense quiet which reigned. They were very
silent when the voices died away.

" If services were conducted in the open air,
we would not be given a jeweller's shop as an
idea of heaven," Penelope suddenly said.

" We all make our own God. The more
spiritual we are, the more spiritually we con-
ceive the Father of the Universe," remarked
Loys.

" Oh, look here, you agnostics, or pantheists,
or whatever you are, I shall leave you if you
begin to discuss religious matters," Kendall
avowed. " Are you a bit the happier for disbelieving what you were taught to believe when

you were children?" He never questioned
certain subjects. "Well, I am glad I still
believe in the old-fashioned heaven."

"'Heav'n but the vision of fulfill'd desire.'
But the believers and the unbelievers are all
more concerned in laying the corner-stones of
their earthly mansions than for those they hope
to occupy beyond the skies," said Yorke. "It
is not so comfortable a creed, but we know we
are independent agents, not puppets, whose
acts must be our own saviour. But as Carlyle
said, 'Not our logical mensurative faculty, but
our imaginative one, is king over us.'"

"And what are Mrs. Kendall's views?"
queried Bedell, raising himself to look at her.
"She has fallen asleep," he announced, in a
whisper, in the tone of one making a wonderful discovery.

"Do not stop talking now," cautioned Yorke,
"or the sudden quiet will waken her."

"I have been sitting so long that my legs
are dizzy," Penelope laughed. "Who wishes
to go for a walk?"

With the exception of Kendall, who preferred
to remain with Loys, and Yorke, who had to
care for the horses, the whole party professed
their readiness to go.

They started out on their tramp, and Yorke went away to feed and water the horses. When he returned a while later, Kendall was sitting beside Loys, ready to brush from her the mosquitoes and flies.

Yorke threw himself down at some distance, but he could see the exquisite care Kendall took of his wife.

After a time Yorke went off for a lonely walk. When he returned, he found Kendall still patiently watching.

" She has not wakened once," Kendall whispered, happily, looking up at Yorke's approach, " and she has been having happy dreams, for she has been smiling."

Loys stirred, then opened her eyes. She was wide awake on the instant.

" How long have I been asleep? I suppose I should be ashamed of myself, but I am not. I feel like another person."

It was after five when they reached the cottage and sat down to dine. Penelope tried to prevail upon them to remain over-night, but only succeeded in inducing Mr. Browne to do so.

After dinner Loys lay in the hammock on the veranda. The others surrounded her, but she did not enter into their merry talk. She

was aware that Van Arsdale was speaking a
great deal, and she appreciated the effort he
was making to create a favorable impression
upon Penelope's friends. She did not doubt
the happiness of Penelope's future, — the world
might believe that her years of waiting were
not justified in him, but the thought would
never occur to Penelope, who had always freely
given more than she could ever hope to receive.

The warm, sweet-scented night-air recalled
to Loys those peaceful evenings Penelope and
she had spent at the cottage the summer before.
She now looked back upon those months as
the happiest she had ever known. The future
had stretched bright before her, and now —

She would not think, when thinking could
lead only to madness. Why, she demanded,
impatiently, why could she not deceive herself
as well as others? Kendall's laugh broke on
the air, and she wondered angrily why she
could not also adopt his brazen indifference
to consequences. A second later she was
conscious of her own inconsistency. She was
thankful that he was not haunted by any
thought of the sword suspended above him.
In his oblivion lay his safety. If his days were
poisoned as hers by the ever-living fear —

The laughter of the others reached her, and she wished she could be as easily moved to laughter again.   And yet she was young ; she was not yet twenty-seven, — almost a year younger than Penelope.   And she might live to be fifty or more.

"Get up, lazy one," commanded Penelope. "Since you persist in going, it is time you prepared."

The train was almost empty.   Opposite them sat a husband and wife, with a child of some four or five years of age.   The child was fractious from sleepiness, and when the mother refused to allow her to hold her head out of the window, the little one set her teeth and began to scream.

"You are to stop that this moment," ordered the mother, shaking the child angrily to and fro.   "I 'll teach you to show such a temper."

Moved as she was to pity the baby, Loys herself could hardly restrain a smile at the ludicrousness of the scene.

"I am surprised that you do not offer to soothe the child for her," mocked Kendall, in French.

"I do not like children, promiscuously," Loys replied, simply.   "They must be sweet and clean, or pretty, or clever. Poor little thing," she added, as the mother continued to scold.

She was glad to escape the child when they went on the ferry. Kendall stood on the deck after the others were seated.

"Come for a walk, Van Arsdale," he urged. "I have not fairly stretched my legs to-day, and I might as well lay the status of that San José matter before you now."

They lighted their cigars and started off, leaving Loys and Yorke together.

In the cabin a harpist and violinist were strumming out the popular music of the day.

"How do you contrive to get along without the song of 'the girl next door'?" asked Yorke.

"Did you not know that they rented the house on the other side of us? I thought you knew, for Penelope made quite a jest of it. They did not own the other property, so there was no need for them to wait until it was re-built. When they took the house adjoining our present location it seemed as if we could not escape the song. But I am glad that we shall miss it soon; we are to return to our own house in a short while now. Do you know, the song has grown sadder than ever."

The musicians had wandered into " Mignon,"
and Yorke began to hum, " Connais-tu le pays,"
but the words faded away on his lips, and he
looked over the motionless, moon-lit waters,
all the unrest of the day dying out under the
calm beauty of the night.

The boat seemed to be scarcely moving
through the silvered waters, in which the stars
were mirrored, and even the wheezing of the
violin could not drown the beauty of the music.

Yorke was facing Loys, who had half-turned
to look back over the bay. As the last note
died away, their eyes met, and their hearts
were laid bare to each other. Her breath
quickened, but she made no attempt to escape
the warmth of his gaze. He bent his head.
His lips had already framed themselves into
the word ' Loys,' when Van Arsdale's voice
broke harshly upon the air.

" Do you wish to be left here all night? "
he demanded, standing at some little distance
from them. " We have landed."

"You are almost asleep, Loys," laughed
Kendall, taking her arm.

She stood up, looking about her vaguely.
An instant later she studied Van Arsdale in
breathless suspense. He had noted nothing:

his face was as blank and expressionless as ever.

Yorke said good-night at the wharf, but Van Arsdale accompanied them to the cars, where he also left them.

Kendall and Loys sat on the dummy.

"You are going to sleep well to-night," he said. "This day in the open air has done you a world of good. Next Friday we shall go to Del Monte, and we shall see if there is not some one there who can induce you to remain a week or two."

"Gregory, can you not leave now? We would go away, just you and I, on a sea-trip to Alaska or Honolulu."

"It is impossible," he decided. "I wish I could, dearest, for I feel you need the change; but it is altogether impossible for me to go now."

"It is not impossible," she protested, with almost hysterical insistence. "Nothing is impossible. I do not make many requests, so you should not refuse me this one. Take me away," she continued, in the suasive tones she could so well employ. "You will find me the merriest companion. You will see how changed I shall be as soon as we are away from here. Will you not take me away?"

Kendall did, indeed, find it difficult to refuse her. She was irresistible as she leaned lightly forward, her dark eyes pleading for her with all their practised skill.

"You make me feel myself a brute," he said, "for I cannot get away now. My darling, do you not see how hard it is for me to refuse you? Do you not know what those weeks would be to me? Here I have to divide you with so many. I never seem to have a moment with you alone. But you who are always so reasonable, you must see that it is out of the question for me to leave now."

"Mother is coming to town to-morrow. I may go home with her."

His eyes widened in surprise. Since her marriage she had gone to the farm only four or five times, and then for but brief stays. She had grown more tolerant of her father's intolerance, but she was always glad to escape from the narrowness of the farm life. Her father had made her several visits of short duration. He was proud of her success, and pleased her by his rough praise, but he was uncomfortable away from the routine of the farm.

"You will stay only two or three days," Kendall hazarded. "Even if not before, I

17

think I can leave in November, and then we shall go to the Islands, or even Japan, if you wish."

"November is a long way off, — almost four months. What cannot happen in four months! Who knows? I may have taken the 'leap into obscurity.' "

"I wish you would stop that senseless talk," he said, harshly. "One would think you took pleasure in the thought of death."

She did not answer. She remembered that long ago, before their marriage, she had once told him that death, to her, seemed a promise of peace. To-night she knew it to be the only peace she would ever gain. She stretched out her hands to it in passionate longing. She would lie at rest, all her fetters fallen from her, free from the feeling of miserable shame which now enveloped her. What a blessed relief it would be no longer to have to pretend to be happy when her heart was heavy with its own shame, when —

"Come, Loys," Kendall's voice broke in. "Here we are at our own door."

Chapter XX

ORKE waited as Van Arsdale paused in the shelter of a doorway to light the cigar, which, in the warmth of his conversation, he had permitted to die out.

"And so," Van Arsdale proceeded, after a luxurious moment of communion with his cigar, "and so, if I were you, I should not wait until September to go on. McIvors is well able to manage your affairs : he is a man of fine executive ability and thoroughly reliable. Why not go to New York this month, and then continue on to England? San Francisco is very well for a man of affairs, and a very Paradise for people of limited means ; but, after all, one merely exists here. You miss the atmosphere to which you have been accustomed, and that last article of yours shows it."

Yorke smiled grimly. "It so happened that it was written in Paris."

"Is it possible?" Van Arsdale queried, not at all disconcerted. "Well, I suppose you will start for New York, then, some time next week."

"I do not know when I shall go," Yorke returned, coldly. He suddenly realized that it was time he left if Van Arsdale could bring himself to prompt the step.

Van Arsdale ventured no further remark. He threw away his cigar, pausing before the Kendalls' door.

"Penelope is with Mrs. Kendall and Mrs. Yerrington. Kendall is at San José, trying that suit. Coming in with me?"

Yorke rapidly decided to enter. It was two days since they had parted at the wharf, and he recognized that it would be well to have their meeting take place before others.

"I am not glad to see you, for I know you have come to take Penelope away," Loys said to Van Arsdale. "And you," she went on to Yorke, "you have come to see my mother, not me."

"We have been speaking of Trent's good-fortune," Penelope observed, after a time. "How much easier it would have been for him had he only been granted a peep into the future! It is much easier to keep up one's courage in the struggle if only assured of ultimate success."

"Perhaps he did consult a clairvoyant," suggested Van Arsdale, gravely. "I have heard that you go to certain mediums, and they liberally give you a number in the lottery which will certainly bring you the capital prize, yet they themselves are content to abide in desolate poverty. Just as the 'beauty doctors' promise you women wondrous beauty if you only entrust yourselves to their hands, yet neglect to beautify themselves."

"You will not mock at clairvoyancy when you hear Mrs. Kendall's experience," warned Penelope. "Loys, tell them what Mrs. Wills told you, — at least as much as you told me."

"You did not go to a fortune-teller, did you?" demanded Mrs. Yerrington, fearfully. "Oh, I am sorry you went. It always seems to me that one gets punished for trying to know."

"So I did; I am sorry I did gratify my unholy curiosity," Loys granted, a furrow of pain crossing her brow. "It was rather a peculiar experience, — my visit to Mrs. Wills. I first heard of her through two of the girls at the school, who were planning to go to see her. Of course, I prevented their going, but I went in their stead. She made no pretension to being a spiritualistic medium; she merely professed to have cultivated her powers of insight. I went to her that day filled with one thought; but almost as soon as she took my hands in hers she told me that I had two sisters, both younger than myself, and she also foretold Laura's marriage in December, which took place."

"That might be reasonably accounted for under the head of mind or muscle reading," remarked Yorke.

"But I was not thinking of my sisters," Loys objected. "As usual, I was thinking of myself."

"Still, they might unconsciously have been in your mind."

"Perhaps. She also told me your name, mother."

Although Van Arsdale had scoffed at the whole idea, he listened with unwaning interest, as did Yorke; but Mrs. Yerrington hung upon Loys's words with breathless impatience.

"Then she told me my occupation. I have often tried to account for that on the presumption that she was a sort of female Sherlock Holmes, but I was exceedingly well-gowned that day; I had no blot of ink on my hands, nor did my face wear the worried expression a teacher's is supposed to have. She also knew that I had written a book, but said

I was too young at the time of writing it. She predicted success for me if I wrote another, yet advised me not to use my eyes at night. I began to work on the story at night, and my eyes rebelled. Of course I cannot tell you all that she foresaw, but it was astoundingly true."

They dared not question her further, although stirred by a violent desire to know how far she had been warned of the future in store for her.

" If you are expecting those people, Penelope, it is time you went home," prompted Van Arsdale.

"Is that clock right? I am sure they are there already. I would much rather stay here than entertain them," Penelope confessed, hospitably.

When Loys returned to the room, after seeing Penelope and Van Arsdale to the door, she found that Yorke had risen to go.

" You made a grave mistake in relating your experience before Mrs. Yerrington," he said. "She is certain that you were told of some trouble in store for you, and that the thought of it is tormenting you."

" Really, mother? I shall tell you two a little secret. I did not mention it before because Mr. Van Arsdale's incredulity irritated me. Mrs. Wills did make one or two mistakes.

It is true she told me your name, mother, at once, but she was extremely puzzled over father's, although she finally gave it to me. She closed her eyes, so," she went on, suiting the action to her words, "and frowned, murmuring, 'Who is this man I see, whose name begins with a J?   It is your father.   J, J — It escapes me.' "

Loys slowly opened her eyes, and confronted her mother, who had risen from her chair.

There was a deathly stillness as the two women faced each other.   Loys drew a dry, gasping breath, and grasped the back of a chair to steady herself.

"I must go," said Yorke.   "Do not trouble to see me out.   I know the way."

But Loys followed him into the hall, closing the door upon her mother.

"You must be lonesome without Gregory," Yorke went on.   "I suppose, however, that he will be away only a few days.   Good-night."

But he did not go.   He stood looking down at her set face.   He could not go away and leave her thus.   He was swayed by a consuming desire to bear her away from those who had heaped one burden after the other upon her young shoulders.   It did not occur to him at that moment that he was thinking of adding to her troubles the weightiest one under which woman ever staggered. He remembered only that they loved each other.

"I am sure you always add a postscript to your letters," she ventured, opening the house-door. She tried to smile, but the smile became a moan.

"Go; for mercy's sake, go."

She had forced upon him the fact that he had no right to console her, and he left her.

She stood leaning against the door. She was suffocated by the tumultuous beating of her heart.

"It cannot be so. I will not have it so," she insisted, passionately. "She shall tell me nothing, nothing."

At length she groped her way back to the room, and noiselessly opened the door.

Mrs. Yerrington was sitting erect in her chair, her eyes looking unseeingly at the opposite wall.

Loys stole nearer and placed her hand upon her mother's arm.

"Come, dear, let us go to bed," she urged.

Mrs. Yerrington turned, looking into Loys's eyes, which petitioned silence.

"What a great deal you have to forgive
your mother," she murmured. "You cannot
understand, for you are a happy wife, and I was
never strong like you, dear. But I'll not say
I am sorry," she continued, fiercely. "Do you
hear, I was happy once for a brief while. I
have paid for it, oh, I have paid for it! You,
you cannot know what I have suffered. Loys,
Loys, my child, my only one, do not say you
cannot forgive me."

Chapter XXI.

AND so it came home to Bishop Yorke that he had been looking with distorted eyes at right and wrong; and when he awoke to a sense of the right he was brave enough to follow it, though all his passions mocked at him. He would go away, and at once; by so doing he would serve Loys best and prove the unselfishness of his love.

There came back to him some words she had said only a few weeks before. He had mentioned some social duty he owed which he felt it irksome to pay, and she had laughed: "Happiness does not always lie through duty's door, does it?"

"It certainly does not this time, so I shall forego the duty," he had replied, easily. "For there is the duty we owe ourselves to be happy, is there not?" he had asked, growing grave.

There had been a short pause before she answered. "I have thought so, too, in rebel-

lious moments, when my reason was beclouded
and I juggled with my conscience. But, after
all, we have both lived long enough to know
that the duty we owe ourselves is to be true to
our higher selves."

"Even at the cost of happiness?" he had
urged, holding her with his eyes.

"Yes, even so," she had said, unflinchingly.

His will must acquiesce with her stronger
one, and he must leave her to fulfil her own
ideas of duty. For himself, he confessed he
was too weak to stay to watch the effort he
knew was a living torment to her. Were he to
stay, the hour would surely come when he would
speak, though knowing full well the only out-
come of it.

Yet at times during that night of preparation
he shrank from the thought of departure, so full
of his great need of her he almost convinced
himself that he had the right to persuade her it
would be better for them to be miserable together than apart. Almost, but not quite; for
though for months she had been in his thoughts
night and day, she had always been peculiarly
aloof from him in a way, despite the note of
appeal in her eyes, which had never died out
since the night he had brought her home, and

which seemed to tell him she relied upon him to be strong for her sake.

The draughts he had drawn upon his strength were visible to Penelope Browning's eyes when he called upon her the following night.

" Of course, as you have fully determined to go, there is nothing more to be said," Penelope remarked. " You always did do exactly what you wished. We shall miss you sadly, as you must know. But you will probably be in New York when we arrive there. When are you going to say ' Good-by ' to Mrs. Kendall? To-night or to-morrow? " There was a note of anxiety in her voice that she could not entirely subdue.

" I suppose to-night," Yorke returned, after a moment's pause.

" If she had not suddenly altered her plans, she would not be home to-night. All along she intended to return with her mother; but although Mrs. Yerrington went home this morning, Loys did not accompany her. I was over twice to-day, but each time the maid said Loys was asleep, having suffered all night from a headache. She expects Gregory home this evening."

She arose in nervous haste and walked to

the window, looking across the lawn to Loys's sitting-room.

"She must be better, for she is sitting by the window. I wonder what she has in her arms," she murmured.

Yorke arose.

"I think I shall go with you," said Van Arsdale.

Yorke looked at him with protesting eyes, but offered no objection.

"I shall not bid you good-by now," said Penelope. "With Riker, I shall see you off."

"I do not know that I shall go to Mrs. Kendall's after all," Yorke declared, hesitating when he found himself in the street.

"You will be busy to-morrow. Come."

They mounted the steps and touched the bell. A moment later they were in the living-room. Loys was in a half-reclining attitude on the couch, which stood before the open window, and was embroidering a napkin. Upon the table beside her lay a beautiful doll, arrayed in long baby clothes.

"Are you not afraid Minerva will make you share Arachne's fate?" questioned Van Arsdale, restraining an exclamation of surprise at her appearance.

Great purple shadows outlined her eyes, and her face was colorless save for the unnatural brilliancy of the lips.

" I only embroider ; I never weave — even spells," she answered, in a languid voice, continuing her work.

" You are not well," exclaimed Yorke.

" I am quite well now, but I have suffered to-day," she allowed.

" I see Baby Blue Eyes must have been visiting you," Yorke said, taking up the doll, but still standing over her, scrutinizing her with anxious eyes.

" I sent for her to dine with me. She is already faithless to your doll. She informed me that she wants a real meat baby. But in default of that she was satisfied to take one of our birds. We had always called him ' Dickey Bird,' but she asked me what Dickey stood for, and began to address the canary as Richard Bird. She told me it would suit him better when he was grown up."

" I suppose that occurred to her on account of Mrs. Underhill's insisting upon our calling the little fellow Frederic," said Van Arsdale. " There will be at least one small person who will miss you, Yorke."

"I have concluded to hasten my plans somewhat," explained Yorke, as Loys raised her startled eyes from her work. "I start for New York to-morrow. From there I expect to continue on to London."

Loys leaned down to pick up the floss she had let fall to the ground, wondering if she had suffered so much that she could feel nothing more, for the news gave her nothing but a slight feeling of relief. She made a stitch or two in silence.

"The news is so very sudden," she finally affirmed, in a level voice, working with determined industry, "that I have ready no little speech. Yet even without it, I think you will know how much we shall miss you."

"You are very kind," he rejoined, haltingly. His throat was so parched that his voice sounded muffled and discordant, and the evenness of her words hurt him. He almost succeeded in convincing himself that it was nothing to her whether he went or stayed.

"You and Penelope will have little time to miss any one from now until after the wedding," reminded Van Arsdale. "And by the time we are fairly off, and you are once again settled in your own home, you and Kendall will be starting off for Japan."

"Oh, yes, we shall be very busy," she agreed, keeping her eyes steadily upon the napkin, in which every now and then she made a few stitches in fitful haste; again her hand would remain motionless, as though she had not the strength to continue working. She was surprised that they did not exclaim at the noise her heart had again begun to make. It seemed to drown her own voice.

"And I hear your book will be on the market in time for the fall trade," Van Arsdale continued, angered by Yorke's silence. "Penelope was telling us of the letter you received from your publishers. You must be very much elated."

"Letter?" she repeated, dazedly. "Oh, yes, the letter. So in October I shall figure before the public again, and dear old Mr. Knight will read the book because I wrote it; and though he never reads any novels but mine, he will expect me to be properly dejected when he points out the weak portions of the story."

Her heart was now leaping with sickening rapidity. She wondered if Van Arsdale was duly appreciating her composure. She sat back, as it were, in her chair, and admired the naturalness of her own performance.

13

She felt a mad inclination to laugh at Yorke as he sat with his eyes bent relentlessly upon her, while he hopelessly tangled the doll's hair with his large hand.

"I can see from the toilet you have made that you are expecting Kendall," Van Arsdale said, now utterly at a loss for words. "Do you remember confiding to us once that you always took special pains with yourself for his home-comings?"

For the first time she noticed that she was darning the monogram instead of embroidering it.

"Did I?" she asked, laughing slightly at her discovery, and looking down at her white gown. "Well, I do. But you must never let him into the secret."

"Let us run away before he comes, Yorke," suggested Van Arsdale, "else we may be tempted into telling."

She put down the napkin as Yorke slowly arose.

The voices of some children who were playing in the street floated in at the open window. "King's-ex," one cried.

She wished she, too, could cross her fingers and give the old childish cry. She needed a momentary pause in which to recuperate her strength.

"'Good-by' is never an easy word to say," said Van Arsdale, now seriously angry at Yorke's continued silence.

"You need not say it here. You know I shall accompany you to the door. Perhaps the next time you come, I shall have set up a footman."

"I am afraid we shall have to journey to Europe if we wish to see Yorke," asserted Van Arsdale. "He holds out no hope of coming here for a long time."

"No; I shall probably not return to San Francisco in many years," Yorke at length said, in a stifled voice.

Loys's eyes dilated. She tried to speak, but only succeeded in giving an unsteady little laugh. She saw that Van Arsdale was anxious to get Yorke away, but she did not attempt to aid him. No one need be jealous of these few last moments.

She was dimly conscious of the fact that Yorke's hand had tightened about her own until her rings were cutting into the flesh, and that his speech was broken. She could see his lips moving stiffly, but there was such a surging in her ears that his words did not reach her. If only the hammering of her heart would cease, that she might hear his last words !

Van Arsdale opened the door, and Yorke released her hand. Then he took it again, and drew it to his lips. She suffered the kiss in silence. If she could but think of something to say, something to keep him there a few moments longer !

Yorke continued to stand over her until Van Arsdale slipped his arm through his and led him down the stairs. At the corner of the street Yorke flung aside Van Arsdale's hand.

"I must see her again," he muttered. "I am going back."

"Are you mad? Have you not brought her suffering enough?" asked Van Arsdale, sternly.

Loys had closed the door and blindly fought her way back to the room.

She resumed her seat by the window, but did not take up her work.

She looked over at the chair Yorke had occupied, and saw his hand again caressing the doll's hair. She had not trusted herself to look at his face. It was stupid not to have taken a last look, to endure through the years, — one last

look at the man to whom love had not meant a
selfish awakening to his own needs.

And so he had passed out of her life, and, as
she had always known, at least one part of Mrs.
Wills's prophecy was not to be fulfilled to the
bitter end. There was to be no tragedy, after
all. She would simply go on trying to satisfy
Gregory, taking an interest in her gowns and
her charities and her writing, and, after a while,
perhaps her heart would cease to weigh so
heavily.

She could not see the clock from where she
sat, but she feared it must be time for Gregory's
arrival. He must not come yet, not just yet!
He must wait until she felt a little stronger, a
little more able to raise her face for his kisses.

She would light the spirit-lamp and have the
water boiling to make the tea.

Life seemed to be made up of nothing but
eating and drinking. She wondered what
Gregory would say if, for once, she neglected
the little attentions to which she had accustomed him. Penelope always said she spoiled
him.

But she would not begin to neglect her duties
now; she was glad to think of them, — it brought
a sense of safety to think that thus far she had

not slighted them. She would light the lamp in a few moments, when the pain in her breast had passed. No one must know how weary she was, how weary she had been for the past months. It was restful there, in the shadowy quiet of the window, listening to the song of the girl next door. It was a sad song, but all music sounded sad at night. She would not complain because that song was more heart-breaking than any other. It was strange that Bishop Yorke had not known the name of the song. Perhaps, some day, when in Milan or Paris, he would hear the music again, and it would recall the evenings spent in their —

And so he was going away. After a while she would grow more accustomed to the thought. It would grow painfully familiar, but just now it did not seem that it could be true. Never to see him again! She pressed her hand to her mouth as though to restrain a cry. If he would return just for a moment, and —

Suddenly the walls of the room began to close in upon her. She could not breathe, they were pressing so tight. And then she became aware that Yorke's strong arms were pushing them back, and she was breathing easily again and could hear the song.

It was kind of him to have returned, she thought, smiling drowsily. Yes, it was very kind of him to hold her up so that she could breathe. Her thoughts were floating, but she could still hold fast to ,the remembrance that he was kind.

A silvery shaft of moonlight slanted athwart her hair. When it had faded away, it had left her face imbued with its own peaceful splendor.

When Yorke reached the house a few moments later, the maid was standing at the door. She stepped aside to admit him.

"I forgot my stick," he explained. "Is Mrs. Kendall still in the sitting-room?"

He opened the door, and closed it behind him before turning to Loys. Then he perceived she was not alone. She was lying back upon the couch, and at her side knelt Penelope, her face bent upon Loys's hands.

His bounding pulses were suddenly stilled. He made a few steps, then paused, leaning heavily against a chair for support.

Penelope looked up, then rose, and walked to him.

"Come," she said, taking his unresisting

hand. "Come, look at her as she lies asleep."

He followed her passively, and, in awe, they stood looking down upon the beautiful serenity of Loys's face. It was a peace which forbade all tears or lamentations.

Not a sound issued from Yorke's lips. His face had grown gray and stone-like. Then he bent down to Loys, whispering, in the tone of one who sues for pardon, "Loys, dear love."

Penelope trembled. If Loys could have heard, she would have been warmed to life by his voice.

Then Penelope touched his arm.

"Do you not understand? She is dead. From my window I watched her death struggle. I think I might have saved her, but I made no move. I was thankful she was to know relief from the relentless pain she had undergone. She had borne too much. It was her heart — Dr. Haswell told Gregory and myself last September; but if she had been happy, she might have lived for years. Do you hear? she is dead."

She sank down again beside Loys, and drew the lifeless hands to her quivering mouth.

"Will you leave me alone with her for a few moments?" Yorke asked, in the same strangely quiet manner. "In the years to come I shall be glad of her dreamless rest, but just now——"

A key was fitted in the house-door, and then footsteps echoed through the hall.

Kendall had reached home.

THE END.